"My name should ring inside you like a bell."

Hope blinked at that. "I didn't even think to ask. Were you just wandering around local chapels today or did you specifically come for me? I'm Hope Cartwright, if that helps. And I don't want to be rude, but I think you have me confused for someone else."

He lounged in the seat beside her and she had the stray thought that no man she'd ever met could have seemed as brutally elegant as this one did.

"You are Hope Cartwright," he said, not as if he was sounding out the name, but as if he was confirming her identity. As if, something in her thought then, he is speaking me into existence. "The woman who was promised to me at her birth and who has instead spent these last years making a mockery of that promise."

She could not seem to breathe. He only shook his head. "Did you really believe that I would allow you to marry another? I am Cyrus Ashkan, Lord of the Aminabad Desert, and what I have claimed will never belong to another. This I promise you."

Innocent Stolen Brides

Married by convenient demand, awakened by passion!

Overlooking the shores of Lake Como, a seemingly perfect high-society wedding is about to take a dramatic and unexpected turn...

As Hope makes her way down the aisle towards her convenient husband-to-be, she finds herself picked up and unceremoniously carried out of the church by a stranger, whose claim on her goes back decades! Once the storm clears, will Hope be able to resist the desert king who stole her away?

Find out in
The Desert King's Kidnapped Virgin
Available now!

Being jilted at the altar is an inconvenience Lionel just won't tolerate. So, the commanding billionaire plucks a replacement bride out of the astounded congregation and demands that she marries him instead!

Read on in
The Spaniard's Last-Minute Wife
Coming next month!

Caitlin Crews

THE DESERT KING'S KIDNAPPED VIRGIN

Recycling programs for this product may not exist in your area.

ISBN-13: 978-1-335-59281-1

The Desert King's Kidnapped Virgin

For questions and comments about the quality of this book, please contact us at CustomerService@Harlequin.com.

Harlequin Enterprises ULC
22 Adelaide St. West, 41st Floor
Toronto, Ontario M5H 4E3, Canada
www.Harlequin.com

Printed in U.S.A.

USA TODAY bestselling, RITA®-nominated and critically-acclaimed author **Caitlin Crews** has written more than a hundred and thirty books and counting. She has a masters and PhD in English Literature, thinks everyone should read more category romance and is always available to discuss her beloved alpha heroes—just ask. She lives in the Pacific Northwest with her comic book–artist husband, is always planning her next trip and will never, ever read all the books in her to-be-read pile. Thank goodness.

Books by Caitlin Crews

Harlequin Presents

Willed to Wed Him
A Secret Heir to Secure His Throne
What Her Sicilian Husband Desires

The Lost Princess Scandal

Crowning His Lost Princess
Reclaiming His Ruined Princess

The Outrageous Accardi Brothers

The Christmas He Claimed the Secretary
The Accidental Accardi Heir

Visit the Author Profile page
at Harlequin.com for more titles.

CHAPTER ONE

HOPE CARTWRIGHT WALKED down the aisle toward her groom, dressed in the requisite white gown and filled with nothing but a sense of relief.

God knew she'd earned it.

Everything is fine, she told herself as she walked. *Everything will be perfectly fine.*

Just as soon as she made it to the altar and said her vows. That was all it would take.

She blew out a breath, not surprised to find it was a bit shaky. And she kept her eyes focused up ahead on the man who stood at the head of the shockingly long aisle in this picturesque Italian wedding chapel, looking as grimly impatient as ever. He wanted this done as much as she did, Hope knew. Because this was the business arrangement they'd both wanted, as cold and calculated as it could get.

She could have been walking into something far more unpleasant, given her options and her desperate situation, and well did she know it. She doubted she'd thought of anything else in any serious way for the past two years.

Hope walked alone because her mother had, in her typical fashion, become so overset by the fact that Hope was actually marrying—*because everyone gets a happy ending except me,* she had sobbed in her childish way, quick to forget the last few years when she could nurse her feelings instead—that she'd drunk herself into something close enough to a stupor.

Except Mignon never lapsed off into an *actual* stupor. That was the trouble. Stupors suggested some measure of silence, and that was not her style. She was a storm, always. Sometimes wild with joy, sometimes distraught, but always and ever a storm. Accordingly, there had been scenes all morning as Mignon had turned Hope's preparations for this ceremony into a saga about Mignon's own choices.

This arrangement was as close to happy as either one of them was likely to get, Hope had tried to tell her. First Mignon had been mad with glee. Then the champagne had gone to her head and she'd simply been mad. Then had come the tears, the French love songs all sung off-key in honor of Hope's late father—Mignon's one true love—and last Hope had looked, Mignon had been passed out in a pile of butter-yellow chiffon, snoring off the bubbly.

Maybe that was as much of a happy ending as Hope could wish for.

She tried to remember what her severe groom had told her the night before when they'd indulged in a rehearsal right here in this ancient chapel that sat up above the sparkling waters of the famed Lake Como in Italy.

It will not do to race down the aisle in an unseemly

haste, he had said in his usual repressive tones after she'd sprinted toward him from the antechamber.

Even if I feel an unseemly haste? she had asked, smiling.

Her husband-to-be was no love match for Hope. *Love* had not entered into the discussions. As such, he was not particularly interested in her smiles. He did not find her amusing, either, as he had made clear on numerous occasions already. Hope was a means to an end for him, that was all.

This was a good thing. Hope liked the fact that he required a service of her. So that she was not the only one selling herself here.

It also helped that he was not repulsive, like so many of the men who had auditioned for this particular role. Hope had wanted an honorable benefactor in the classic style. Someone she could rely upon and even feel safe with. Maybe there would even be some affection, in time.

Maybe it wasn't the charming fairy-tale prince she'd dreamed of when she was small, but if she'd learned anything since her father died, it was that life was not kind to childish dreams. Looking for a more businesslike arrangement that benefited her as well as the man in question seemed a practical and even lovely alternative, in its way.

Instead she had discovered that entirely too many men out there were nothing short of horrible.

Like the one who had called what she was doing a *virginity auction.* She had been at some pains to tell him that there was no *auction*, thank you. That such a notion was unpleasant and, anyway, not true.

What *was* true was that Hope was, indeed, a virgin. That, like so many things in her life, had been an accident, not any sort of morality crusade on her part. It was a twist of fate, nothing more. If her father had not died when Hope was barely turned fourteen, she imagined she would have had the same kind of adolescence her old friends at school had enjoyed. Silly parties and boys to giggle over instead of having to act as the adult she wasn't. Because Mignon, as delightful as she was most of the time, was sadly incapable of behaving like the adult she actually was with any regularity.

It had been down to Hope to sort out the funeral, then all the bills that followed. To do the best she could with the money her father had left and her mother's seeming determination to blow through it all at an alarming rate as she dealt with her terrible grief. Hope had been the one who'd sold off the family estate, sorrowfully parting with her father's staff, who had all been there longer than her, because she could not afford to keep them on. It had been Hope who had found the two of them a flat in London that Mignon wailed about on some maudlin evenings, because the neighborhood was questionable—Hope liked to think of it as *up-and-coming*—and what would people *think*, and what was next, the *poorhouse*?

Mignon kept clinging to the hope that even one of the men who partied with her, took advantage of her, or used her as they wished might love her if she let them [illegible]

They never did.

And so it was Hope who had to save them.

That was how she'd come to the attention of far too many obnoxiously wealthy and self-involved men since she'd turned eighteen. Her birthday present to herself, such as it was, had been leaving Mignon singing into her wine to meet her first potential contender. Hope had used her father's connections to put herself forward, but only to a very specific sort of individual. He needed to be rich, first and foremost, because while she felt that she might quite like to make her own way in the world, what mattered was that Mignon would want for nothing.

That was what Hope's dad would have wanted. No matter what flights of fancy her mother might commit herself to. No matter what Hope did or didn't do.

That was what Hope wanted too, because she loved her mother. And she understood, somewhere deep inside, that she had a certain grit her mother lacked. She had a fortitude while Mignon was made of pretty smiles and too much air. She had no head for reality.

Reality had been Hope's father's job.

Mignon needed looking after, that was the beginning and end of it. In return, Hope was prepared to sign anything. Any prenuptial agreement, any contract, anything at all. After two years out there on what only an optimist like her mother would call "a dating scene," Hope had *almost* convinced herself that she was well and truly prepared to be the virgin sacrifice she had learned a certain kind of man dreamed of finding.

After all, she had but two things that she could use to her advantage, according to far too many of the unpleasant men she'd encountered, having had to forgo any A levels to leave school at sixteen to take care of her mother as best she could: her father's august pedigree and the fact that Hope herself was entirely untouched.

Sometimes she almost thought it was funny, that the thing her friends had teased her about in the years since her father's death had become the only weapon Hope had, it seemed. The only possible way she could get *both* herself and her mother out of this mess.

Though she had taken her time coming to that conclusion, because it was so medieval.

Because she could always get a job, she'd told herself at first, the way normal people did. She sometimes thought about a glorious *career* the way she imagined some people dreamed of beach vacations in the Spanish sun. But the trouble was, Mignon could not do the same. Several attempts on her part had proved that, until Mignon had been forced to confess that she thought she was, perhaps, an idiot missing its village. Which had broken Hope's heart.

In my dreams I am a fierce warrior for you, Mignon had whispered, working hard to keep a tremulous smile on her lovely, tearstained face. *While in reality I am a mess. Beyond redemption, I fear.*

No. Hope had been certain. Fierce. *Never that.*

That had left Hope to set aside any lingering Prince Charming fantasies—as well as any notions of a career, for that matter—and attempt to find a decent job that could support her *and* her mother when Hope had no work experience as well as no advanced education. But that was fine. She was scrappy. And while she had feelings, she was not buffeted this way and that by them, like Mignon.

She viewed this as a superpower, really.

But regardless of her feelings, and whether or not they ruled her, it had been a grueling two years of "dating" the sort of men who she found increasingly and almost unbearably unpleasant as time went on. Which was deeply unfortunate, as her dwindling funds made her more and more desperate to find someone—anyone—to help them, and running out of money meant she was running out of options.

Because one after another, the terrible men who took her out to such seemingly elegant dinners confessed their darkest and most furtive fantasies to her as if she'd *asked* for such intimate details, making it impossible for Hope to agree to any terms they might put to her.

One after the next, they made it impossible to do the thing she knew she had to do to save her mother.

And when she refused them, they took great pleasure in making it clear that her virginity was her only currency, and her pedigree a mere gloss to go with it.

She began to fear that sooner or later, she would have to marry one of them and do whatever their vile imaginations conjured up, somehow.

Two years ago, Hope had foolishly believed that she would find the perfect solution to all her problems, and quickly.

After all, she'd started her search for the proper benefactor by aiming straight for men her father's age, many of whom she'd met when she'd been a little girl. The men who she'd known had precious little in the way of scruples. Because she knew precisely which ones had taken it upon themselves to offer her mother what they called *comfort*, while drooling, after the funeral.

Instead, she'd had two years of exploring precisely how twisted and appalling some men really were.

A lesson she would have preferred not to learn at all, though she supposed it was good she had. Since there were *so many* of them.

Lionel Asensio had been a breath of fresh air, she thought now, because it was good to remind herself of reality. And the fact she'd survived those two years without succumbing to those revolting suggestions she had found so impossible to imagine, much less imagine *doing.* She kept her eyes trained on him as she continued down the aisle, reminding herself further that this was an escape today. A victory. Because his notice of her had been a solution.

Finally, the kind—if cold—benefactor she'd been seeking all along.

Lionel Asensio had his own reasons for marrying in cold blood and in such haste. Hope did not care what those reasons were—she was merely delighted that he had them. She'd felt nothing but relief when he had actually wanted the gilt and gloss of her father's spotless pedigree. That the fact that the Cartwrights stretched back through the ages ever since the original cart-making owner of the name had been elevated from his humble origins by a long-dead queen had intrigued him the most. Even her mother had helped in that respect, for Mignon had been raised in a family that seemed unaware that there was no longer the sort of French aristocracy that had once led to any number of revolutions. She had been made to shine brightly, that was all, and that was what she did. From her still-pretty face straight down into her thoroughbred bones.

All of this had impressed Lionel Asensio.

Her innocence had not been part of the initial discussions at all.

And none of that mattered today. Today was a day to walk very, very slowly down this aisle and congratulate herself on her own grit, not worry overmuch about terrible men or once noble blood. Mignon was even now sleeping off the morning's excesses and would no doubt rise to dance again later this afternoon, flushed and happy that her daughter had wrangled the only thing Mignon had ever wanted in life—a husband.

As she walked without any undue haste, Hope was actually entertaining the notion of getting some kind of job after all. The wife of a billionaire like Lionel Asensio could create charities with a wave of her hand. She wouldn't have to worry about not having the proper qualifications to work in the nearest chip shop.

Hope could hardly wait to see what she was *actually* good at. Not what she was *forced* to do instead.

All it would take were a few vows. A few signatures on the contracts she'd already read over and agreed to verbally. So little, in the end, to be free at last. Really, her stone-faced husband-to-be was lucky she hadn't sprinted down the narrow stone aisle to get on with things more quickly, which she suspected he would find unseemly in every regard.

There weren't many people here today, which Hope

was happy about, because this wasn't exactly an all-out celebration of whatever a wedding usually celebrated. *Fairy tales*, she thought, but not *wistfully*. She'd learned her lesson there. *Wistfulness* was about as useful as childhood fantasies about far-off princes and castles made of stone. She thought the entirety of the congregation, sparse as it was, were members of Lionel's staff—with the exception of one woman in the back, who was scowling from behind big glasses and looked like a library was missing its fearless leader. She entertained herself for a few slow steps by imagining that was a special guest of the groom, who might very well have hidden bookish depths that required a personal librarian on call, for all Hope knew.

What she did know for certain was that Lionel himself was a man of some renown, as most people in his tax bracket were. Wealth created its own legends, she had discovered over the past two years. She had been subjected to a great number of meetings with his PR team once she and Lionel had come to an agreement. They had decided how to fashion this strange wedding into a palatable romantic tale that could sell newspapers, appease the ever-nosy public, and serve Lionel's own ulterior motives.

Hope didn't care about any of that.

All she wanted was to get this over with, so that she could move at last into the next phase of her life. Maybe let herself grieve the loss of her father at last, now that she wasn't forced to deal with the fallout of losing him.

While she was at it, she planned to pay off the last of her mother's creditors and set up pensions for the loyal staff she had been forced to let go when she'd sold the family estate. She had promised them that if it was ever within her power, she would do exactly that. She'd been flattered back then that they'd pretended to believe she might when she hadn't believed it herself.

Now she could prove, at last, that she was more her father's daughter than her mother's. She loved them both, she truly did, but she did not want to think of how scared her mother had been these past few years. She did not like remembering how Mignon had sobbed and sobbed, too aware that her attempts to help only made things worse.

Hope had no intention of letting circumstances wreck her like that. Ever.

And she was imagining how good it would feel, to take care of the people who had always taken care of her—and walking slower than a snail, God help her, because it made political sense to obey her almost-husband's instructions as soon as she could—when there was a sudden great noise from the back.

Hope froze, her eyes closing of their own accord.

That would be her mother, no doubt. And there was no way Mignon could have slept off all that champagne and sobbing, so she would be wilder than usual—

Up at the head of the aisle, she saw the way her groom's jaw tensed, and she couldn't have that. Not until they were well and truly married, and all of this was done.

Never had she wanted to break into an impolite sprint for the altar more than she did just then, but Hope turned instead. She expected to find Mignon staggering toward her in some or other questionable state. Or dancing down the aisle, singing French lullabies.

She opened her mouth as she turned, prepared to try to redirect her mother, but Hope found herself unable to speak at all because it wasn't her mother who strode toward her.

It was a vision.

Her first impression was of light and heat. A kind of mad explosion that seemed to take place entirely within her.

It took her long, jarring moments while her heart clawed its way out of her chest to understand that what she was looking at was a man.

But he was like no man she had ever beheld.

And she had spent these past two years becoming something of a reluctant expert on the species. This man was…not like the others.

This man walked as if his footsteps upon the ground were a favor he was doing for the stone floor beneath him and, perhaps, the earth itself. He was very tall, and though he was dressed in the sort of exquisite suit that could have made any form look perfect, she had an immediate and innate understanding that there was no sleight of hand here. His shoulders were truly that wide. He was *actually* made of all that muscle, lean and hard, and every step he took made it clear that unlike the sorts of men that Hope was used to, he used his body for hard, physical things.

Hard, physical things, she whispered to herself, a hot little echo that seemed to send a kind of too-bright, glittering burst straight through her.

But more than all of that—though *all of that* was a lot—he was dangerous.

She could feel that danger like a new, intense heat, like flames breaking out from the nave and taking over the whole of the church. And the strangest sensation swept over her, like her own skin had simply burst out all over into that same kind of fire. She would not have been at all surprised to find flames dancing up and down her arms, part of that fire that climbed and climbed, hotter and higher, the longer she looked at him.

Hope had some odd thought that perhaps he was a guest who had merely come late, that perhaps he knew Lionel somehow—

But even as she thought it, she realized that he was focused on her.

Only on her.

That meant she could do nothing at all but stare at him in return.

This was not a hardship, but her body reacted as if it was a *hard, physical thing* all its own. He had eyes of an unholy midnight in a face sculpted from bronze. He had a blade of a nose, dark brows, and a mouth so stark it made something inside her feel hollow, as if overwhelmed with the austerity she saw there.

So overwhelmed it made her shiver, and not because she was cold.

He bore down upon her and Hope knew on some level that it could only have taken a few seconds. His strides were so long, so deliberate. It could only have been one breath, maybe two, but it felt like an eternity.

An eternity of gazing at this man, this apparition,

and all of that light and heat. An eternity of a kind of wonder as one explosion fed into the next inside her, making new and strange sensations burst into life all over her skin and then reach deep in her core.

An eternity that felt like fate.

Like a deep recognition when she was more certain than she had ever been of anything that she had never laid eyes on this man before.

An eternity—

But then he was *right there* before her.

And the whole world seemed to tilt and whirl, knocking her so far off its axis she felt as if she was spinning off into space—

It took her far too long to understand that he had lifted her up, tossing her over his shoulder as he spun around to march right back up that aisle again.

It took her too long because once again, all of that impossible sensation seemed to detonate inside of her.

That hard, muscled shoulder was making itself known against her belly with every step. Worse—*better?*—his hand was on her bottom, holding her fast.

She was reduced to a shiver with head dangling down against the hard stretch of his muscled back.

Surely she ought to…fight this, or something, she thought, but she felt no particular *urge* to do anything of the kind.

And she couldn't tell if anyone else was protesting—not when there was far too much ringing in her ears and a mad noise in her head. But by the time the thought landed in her, fully formed, they were already outside. She could feel the sweet Lake Como breeze that seemed to press against her face, making it clear to her that she was already far too hot for anything like comfort.

The man kept going, stalking away from the chapel and down the narrow old road—really more a path—that she'd walked up not long ago.

Hope felt dizzy and outside herself—yet no matter how she tried to lecture herself, she couldn't quite bring herself to cause a scene. To shout, make demands, or attract attention.

Everything shifted again, a rush and tumble. And she could hardly make sense of that, either, until he slid into the back of the vehicle where he'd tossed her, slammed the door behind him, and said something in a foreign language to another man at the steering wheel in front.

A foreign language that was neither the Italian a person would expect to hear while in Italy nor even the Spanish that was her almost-groom's first language.

She should have been terrified. Yet as the vehicle lurched away, Hope found herself blinking back the strangest rush of an emotion that certainly wasn't fear.

Relief, something in her pronounced, and though she told herself it was an accusation, it didn't feel like one.

Because if she was being spirited away, against her own wishes and without her own advanced knowledge or direction, she couldn't be expected to go through with her wedding, could she?

Deep down, she could admit that delighted her, because she didn't really want to marry Lionel.

Or anyone else.

And, sure, this felt a great deal like a frying pan into the fire moment, but if she had learned anything in these last, difficult years, it was that she should always take time to mark the little victories. No matter what.

Because they were few and far between, and needed celebrating when they came.

Mignon had taught her that.

"Do not attempt to escape," the man beside her told her as if she'd lunged for the door. It made her think she should have tried, at the very least, for appearances' sake. Especially because she couldn't quite *look* at him. Not directly. He was too.... beautiful, yes, in a harsh kind of way that made her think of a storm. As implacable as he was stunning, and she found she had no place to put that.

"We will be in the air within the hour," the man continued in that same forbidding way that she really shouldn't have found so...*compelling.* "Nothing and no one will stop us. And anything but the strictest obedience on your part will be met with consequences I doubt very much you will like."

"Well," Hope said, mildly enough, looking down at her hands. She thought her hands ought to have been shaking, though they weren't, and moved them against the skirt of her gown to feel its smoothness against her palms. She had gone for very little adornment because even the faintest embellishment had felt romantic and this wedding had been a business arrangement, nothing more. "That's me told, then."

Beside her, she could feel the man shift, and was aware of his affront even before she glanced over to confirm it.

"This is who you are," he said in a low voice that

was rich with a kind of betrayal that made her stomach flip, even though she couldn't understand it. Not from a stranger. "You do not even care what man claims you, do you? You flit from one to the next as if it is nothing."

"This was a bit less of a flit," she pointed out, trying to focus slightly to one side of his outrageously handsome face because all of that hard bronze was too distracting. "And a bit more of a kidnap, really. So it's not exactly sporting to hold me responsible for it, is it?"

And it was only as she said that out loud that the truth of what was happening really rushed through her, like some floodgates had opened deep within. When Hope hadn't even known that she *had* floodgates. She would have said that all such emotion had been carved out of her years ago.

That's just what happens when you're desperate, she told herself tartly.

In her desperation, Lionel had seemed like a savior. He was not unpleasant. He was not even unkind. He was businesslike all the way through and his wanting to marry her saved her from far worse fates. Hope knew that well enough, though she hadn't wept with joy when she'd agreed to marry him the way her mother had. But she could admit that she'd felt some measure of peace, and even happiness that she'd managed it. That she'd saved Mignon.

And herself in ways she hadn't imagined she'd need to when she'd started this journey two years ago.

But at least she'd *agreed* to her deal with Lionel. She hadn't agreed to *this*.

"You are mine," the man beside her told her then.

"You will spend what remains of your life in the palm of my hand. And your behavior alone will dictate whether my hand remains open or closed up tight, like a fist. But hear me now that this will be the only choice remaining to you."

Hope nodded along, the way she'd learned to do when powerful men spoke, only realizing when he frowned at her that this was probably not the correct response. Not when he was very clearly issuing a threat.

Because it was most certainly a threat, she had no doubt about that.

What this man did not seem to understand was that she had creditors whose threats were far more concrete.

"I can see that I'm supposed to cower," she said then, helpfully. "But if I can be honest here, is there any way we could just skip this part and get to what you actually want from me? It's only that I had a very dramatic morning. And as much as I appreciate being carried off from a wedding I wasn't exactly thrilled with in the first place, I really am going to have to go back. There is my mother to consider."

The frown on the man's beautiful, arrogant face had turned into an open scowl that deepened with every word. "You are never going back. Was I unclear?"

"You were perfectly clear. It's just that it won't work," Hope told him, matter-of-factly. "It's not you. This is really a wonderful kidnap. Very overwhelming, I promise you. It's only that I'm pretty much dead inside, so I'm afraid that mustering up tears and caterwauling and whatever else you might have been expecting is beyond me. And again, there is my mother to consider. There is always my mother, you see. I love her. And I promised."

She thought of the fond way her father had gazed at Mignon and how he'd said, his voice so affectionate, that one day he hoped that Hope would love her and care for her when he couldn't. *I always will,* Hope had assured him, because she had always wanted to do anything and everything her father wanted. And because she'd loved her delightful, always happy and usually silly mother beyond reason.

Beside her, the man was silent for a moment—but in a way that she could only think of as *thunderstruck.* And not in a good way.

"Do you know who I am?" he asked, his voice a bare ribbon of sound.

"I don't think anyone asks that question and expects the answer to be no," Hope said apologetically, "but no. I don't know who you are. Should I?"

"My name should ring inside you like a bell," he told her, his voice seeming to fill the whole car. "I should be the only thing you see when you close your own eyes. The barest hint of my approval should be the sun your whole earth moves around."

Hope blinked at that. "Goodness. That's…specific indeed." She tilted her head to one side. "I didn't even think to ask. Were you just wandering around local chapels today or did you specifically come for me? I'm Hope Cartwright, if that helps. And I don't want to be rude, but I think you have me confused for someone else."

He lounged in the seat beside her and she had the

stray thought that no man she'd ever met could have seemed as brutally elegant as this one did. He was dressed like any of them, so it wasn't his clothes. It was something about him. He was wrapped up in a kind of ferocity that made all of her nerve endings seem to *sing out*.

And keep right on singing.

"You are Hope Cartwright," he said, not as if he was sounding out the name. But as if he was confirming her identity. *As if*, something in her thought then, *he is speaking me into existence.* When it was her mother who lived by the Lewis Carroll rule to think of at least six impossible things before breakfast, not Hope. "The woman who was promised to me at her birth and who has instead spent these last years making a mockery of that promise."

She could not seem to breathe. He only shook his head. "Did you really believe that I would allow you to marry another? I am Cyrus Ashkan, Lord of the Aminabad Desert, and what I have claimed will never belong to another. This I promise you."

And despite herself, Hope felt those words inside her.

Very much like a single bell ringing, low and deep.

But she shoved that aside, because there was nothing in her life that left any space for *bells*. Or this man with eyes like midnight and the way he looked at her, as if he had yanked her out of the life she knew and into some solar system where there was only him.

What did it say about her that she found the notion… oddly comforting?

Hope didn't know, because everything always came

back to the same place. Some people got to spend their twenties wafting about in search of various identities to try on and discard. They got to take the geographic tour, moving from one place to another, one job to another, one party to the next. Always betting that by process of elimination alone, they might figure out what to *do* with their lives.

Yet Hope had never had that option.

So she smiled at the impossible blade of a man beside her as if nothing could touch her or bother her—not even her own abduction.

"You can claim me all you like," she told him calmly enough, even as the car raced away from Lake Como. "That sounds great, actually. But I will require that we carve out certain concessions in any contracts we sign. That's as a baseline." He seemed to stare at her without comprehension, and somehow, it seemed perilous to keep going. But she did. "Mostly it involves allowances for my mother. Nothing too onerous, I assure you."

The car had been careening through the narrow roads of the Italian countryside, but it stopped now, in the middle of a field where a huge helicopter sat. Hope didn't have to ask if it was his. She knew it was.

She waved a hand at the sleek machine as if she didn't know or care that it would fly her away from Italy and there was precious little she could do about it. Part of her was glad of it, if she was honest. She even smiled a bit wider. "Especially not for man who has one of these on call."

And Hope wasn't at all prepared for what happened

inside her when all Cyrus Ashkan, Lord of some desert, did was laugh.

As if she belonged to him after all.

CHAPTER TWO

SHE WAS MORE compelling than he'd expected and Cyrus Ashkan did not care for surprises.

He arranged his entire life to make certain there were precious few.

In the case of Hope Cartwright, the insult had already been delivered. Accordingly, he had already decided exactly who and what this woman was to him.

He did not like the part of him that wondered if there might be another path, despite everything, now that he had finally met her.

Cyrus had not expected to find so much mystery in her gaze. He had not expected that lifting her into his arms to toss her over his shoulder would *grip* him the way it did. So much so that he could still feel his sex responding to her as if she were his lover instead of merely his possession—not even a prisoner.

For how could he imprison what was already his?

He had expected the gleaming blonde hair, like strands of competing gold in sunlight. He had expected her general comeliness, for he had studied it in too many photographs to count—but in person, she was…something else.

Something unexpected, damn her.

There was a surprising hint of steel about her, as if beneath the pretty picture she made and her sort of English rose loveliness—exactly what he had taught himself to hate, as it reminded him of his own mother's softness and the childhood he had long ago disavowed—her architecture was as unyielding as his.

He dismissed that immediately, of course.

But no matter what it was, or wasn't, she surprised him.

As did her curious defiance. He had expected wailing, temper tantrums, tears.

He had not expected…this quiet negotiation. This total lack of fear. The notable absence of any apparent guilt that she had turned her back on the promises her father had made and the deal he had made with Cyrus's grandmother, for the Kings of the Aminabad Desert had always wedded in this way.

If he didn't know it to be impossible, Cyrus would be tempted to imagine she truly did not know who he was to her.

But that was absurd.

He reached over and wrapped his hand around one slender wrist, disliking intensely the way so simple a touch exploded within him. Her skin was too soft. And there was the sense of some kind of innocence about her that he knew was a lie, no matter how he might wish it otherwise.

"Come," he growled at her.

She only smiled. That did not help.

Because his sex did not seem to know the truth of her when he was afraid he knew it all too well. But then, Cyrus was King of a harsh and unforgiving land. He was not ruled by any man alive and he did not take direction from his sex, either.

He was still laughing at the very idea as he tugged her from the car. He marched her over to the black helicopter that waited there for his next command, then led her inside. They would fly north to Germany where one of his jets waited, and only then would they fly out to the deserts he called his own.

Leaving enough international smoke and mirrors behind them that her would-be husband, a man of no small wealth in his own right, could not hope to find them.

He expected her to pitch a fight as he ushered her into her seat as the rotors began to spin, but she didn't. Instead, Hope came along in a manner he could only describe as *happy.*

As if she could think of nothing better to do on her wedding day then participate in her own abduction.

That, too, was not what he'd expected.

Cyrus told himself that this meant only that she was far more treacherous than he'd imagined. For surely she was recalibrating, that was all, and intended to try her hand at negotiating with him further. As if contracts had not been signed years ago.

But as the helicopter took off, shooting up from Lake Como and carrying her away from the site of her latest bit of perfidy, she didn't seem the slightest bit concerned. She didn't look back at the scene of what would have been the ultimate betrayal—longingly or otherwise. She didn't even fire questions at him.

Hope simply sat in her seat, folded her hands in her lap, and then closed her eyes.

Very much as if she was taking a nap.

Cyrus sat beside her and seethed.

But then, he had been seething for two years now, because he held the vows he made as sacred. If he did not, he would have married long ago instead of waiting for the bride he had been promised. He was owed this debt.

Though she had not been meant to come to him until she was either of age or out of university, he had imagined that once her father died she would reach out to the man she been given to and ask for his aid. She had not.

And then, when she had finally turned eighteen, she had embarked on an enterprise he could only assume had been directed right at him.

She had delivered insult upon insult. A lesser man might very well have taken personally the stain upon his name, but Cyrus was a benevolent lord. That didn't mean this woman who had been promised to him might not wish for a great many different avenues of deliverance all the same.

Because he was owed a debt and he was calling it in.

Her eyes remained closed beside him, but Cyrus stared down at the land below him as the helicopter flew north, low over the mountains and across parts of Switzerland and Liechtenstein before making its way into Germany.

He wanted no part of this place.

He preferred the stark honesty of the desert sands,

as he had been well taught. The simplicity of the life that could, at any moment, be snatched back by the elements. A life where softness was nothing short of deadly. His father had hammered this point into him, again and again.

A place where kings had always ruled and always would.

Cyrus had taken the sins of his mother, each and every one trotted out before him by his father who claimed she had betrayed him, and used them as a cautionary tale. He had allowed the tumult of his early life to teach him and he never took the lessons he had learned at his ruthless father's side for granted.

Indeed, those lessons had always been and would always be his guide in all things.

To this day, he counted himself grateful that he had been saved. That his had not been a destiny of betrayal and boredom like the too-soft woman who had dared attempt to steal him from his father when he was still a boy.

Even if it astonished him that the woman beside him now, the Englishwoman he would never have looked at twice had it not been tradition that he honor his grandmother's promises, did not seem to know that vows in his part of the world were like iron. They did not, could not bend.

But he would show her.

Whether she liked it or not, she would learn.

Just as he had, long ago.

In Germany, the weather was wet and much colder than in Italy. He spoke to his men in a low voice as he climbed out onto the tarmac and ushered his stolen bride toward the jet that waited for him there.

"Gassed and ready to take you home, sire," his man told him in their language.

"Not soon enough," Cyrus growled in reply.

Once again, he expected her to cry foul. To put up some kind of fight or offer some measure of defiance. But she didn't.

Hope simply let him tug her along, almost as if she didn't care where she was going or with whom.

He laughed at that, too, though it was a sound devoid of amusement—because she would learn. There were any number of so-called men littering the cobblestone streets of these European cities. There were men everywhere, all of them making their claims to some power or another, as men always did.

But there was only one Lord of the Aminabad Desert. There was only one Cyrus Ashkan.

And well would this woman come to know what it cost to defy him.

He had not expected to want her at all, though he'd intended to do his duty, as always. He'd expected that her offenses would mark her unattractive in his eyes no matter how pretty she was, but that did not appear to be the case.

It was not that she didn't offend him, of course. She did. She wore a wedding gown, had been walking down an aisle in a chapel to marry another man. How could he be anything but offended?

The trial was that he still wanted a taste. And the

fact that she was not behaving the way he'd expected she would only made it worse.

"Sit and prepare yourself for takeoff," he ordered her curtly once they boarded. "We will not stop until we reach the desert."

He did not specify *which* desert as, to him, there was only and ever one.

"How delightful," she chirped as she swept to the seat he indicated. "I've only ever been to Marrakesh, where one is always going on about the desert without ever actually sticking a toe in the sand."

And if she noticed his scowl at her temerity, she ignored it.

Cyrus settled himself and then watched her closely as the plane taxied down the runway, then made its smooth jump into German airspace. He studied her for clues as the plane made a slow, lazy turn to head south. Hope sat in the seat opposite him, her hair clipped back by some or other set of quietly elegant jewelry and that white dress gleaming.

Like a reminder. Like another insult.

Not that he needed his memory jogged on that score.

He waved a hand when the plane steadied on its course, and his attendants hurried to set out the in-flight meal he normally preferred. A selection of meats and hard cheeses, the fragrant flatbread his people made in the heat, and the filo dough tarts stuffed with something sweet. He indicated the plate before her when all Hope did was stare down at it.

A lot like she'd never seen a meal before.

"Let me guess," he said, and he did not try particularly hard to keep the censure from his voice. "Like so many women, you prefer to starve yourself for attention."

"Oh, I would love to starve myself," the impossible woman replied. And she seemed to mean it, it had to be said. "I've tried and tried. It turns out that I don't really have the knack. I've always preferred to eat my feelings whenever possible."

Then, as he watched in no little astonishment, she dipped the flat, dull knife the attendants had provided her into the pots of butter and jam, slathering both all over the flatbread before her. And then, holding his gaze with an insolence that left him rigid in astonishment, she took an enormous bite.

More, she then seemed wholly unfazed as they both sat there while she chewed and chewed, even having press her fingers over her lips to keep the enormous portion of bread and butter and jam within.

Like a child, Cyrus thought.

But the true outrage was that his body did not consider her any kind of child. Not in any respect.

He thought that would be the end of her games. He assumed that at any moment she would show some sign that she understood the precariousness of her position here, but glare at her though he might, she continucd to eat her fill.

With what looked a great deal like pure, unselfconscious delight.

And only when she cleared the plate before her, filled it again, and then picked her way through the better part of the tray besides did Hope sigh happily and sit back in her seat. Fell back, more like, he thought darkly as she sighed again.

With every appearance of deep and total contentment, one hand slung over her middle.

"I can't remember the last time I really ate anything," she confided, as if he had inquired. "Left to my own devices I would make sure to keep my stomach full at all times, because I do tend to act out when I'm hungry, but my mother wouldn't hear of it when there were dress fittings to consider. I feel as if I've been fasting for weeks."

"Nerves?" But unlike every last one of his men and most of his subjects, Hope did not react to the ice in his voice with instant obedience and respect. "I hear they are common in brides."

That languid hand made a line through the air between them. "Hardly. Or not the way you mean, I think. It's just that managing my mother takes a good bit of effort and it can sometimes be difficult to slot in meals around her."

And Cyrus was hailed far and wide for his ability to see the truth of a man at a glance. To know the truth of whoever dared face him, no matter how unpleasant or hidden. Because of this, he had maintained a constant peace with his neighbors no matter how many new rulers rose and fell in those lands. Aminabad ever remained.

This was one of his great talents in this life, this discernment that had served him so well while he ruled. But he could not, for the life of him, make any sense at all of the girl before him.

Instead he found himself noticing tiny, unimportant details that he should have considered beneath him. Meaningless details, like the fact that her eyes seemed laced with gold and seemed far more intriguing than the more prosaic shade of muddy hazel he had expected. It was the way they shone, perhaps. As if she carried untold treasures inside of her.

He was, equally, not best pleased with the curve of her cheek or the way her lips tipped upward, making it look as if she was smiling all the while. No doubt smug and happy in her many betrayals.

And then there was that curvy figure of hers. She was not one of those lean, willowy tree trunks—much like his reedy mother, betrayer though she was, and that whole side of his family, though he did not like to think of his childhood years at her side—that some men found so attractive. Hope was a lush little creature with the kind of hips real men appreciated. Not only because they suggested a woman would bear children well.

She possessed the wide hips and ripe breasts that enhanced pleasure, and childbearing was secondary to such pursuits. His own palms itched to test the weight of the breasts she wore strapped into the bright white bodice of her gown. And though her waist nipped in, it only made him want to span the width of it with his hands, then see how the flare of her hips felt in his grip.

He had not expected this overwhelming *need* for her. He was having some trouble accepting that he could not brush it aside as he did so many of the things he desired in this life, second always to the demands of his people, his position.

For no reason he could fathom, he remembered how he had once yearned for his mother when he had been taken from her so suddenly, and the way she had always sung to him, crooning and nonsensical songs she made up as she went—

But over time he had turned his back on nonsense and found reason instead.

He no longer permitted himself childish things, and yearning was one of them.

"Have you no questions?" he demanded when he decided he had glared at her long enough, the ferocity his voice a shock to his own ears. The fact that Hope did not seem to notice only kept him on edge. "Do you accept, so easily, simply being removed from your life? On such a day as this?"

"What would you have me do?" And though her tone was easy, there was that hint of something flinty in her golden gaze. It reminded him that she was not so easygoing as she pretended. "Should I have wrestled with you, a man who must outweigh me by some hundred pounds? There in your vehicle, or here, surrounded by your men? Have would that go for me, do you think?"

He didn't like how rational that was. "And so instead you simply…accept your lot? I had no idea you were so meek, Hope. I find myself even more deeply amazed that you took it upon yourself to break the contract between your family and mine."

She took a moment to study him then, and he should have found that satisfying. Surely, at any moment, he would see a dawning awareness break over her features. Then it would begin, he told himself. She would beg him for mercy. He would give it, though he did not intend to forgive her.

"Forgiveness is for the weak," his father had thundered at him, again and again.

Which was not to say Cyrus did not wish to hear her excuses, for he did.

But instead she only lifted a shoulder, a gesture so disrespectful that she was lucky that his men were not here to see it.

"I know of no contract between your family and mine," she told him. Dismissively, if his ears did not deceive him. "But then again, I don't know who your family is. Still, if there were contracts lying about, I would have seen them. Assuming when you say *my family* you mean my father." Then she laughed. "What I'm certain of is that no one attempted to make a contract with my mother. For anything. Might as well throw stones at the moon, and between you and me, you'd get-ter better results that way."

Though she sounded almost…indulgent, to his ears.

"I have told you who I am." And there was something in Cyrus then, far more wintry and frozen than a man of the desert should have been capable of. "My father was Lord of the Aminabad Desert before me, though I believe he was more commonly known as King Hades in your gutter press."

"King Hades." She repeated the name, then blinked. And then, as he had known she would, she sat up straighter, her head cocking to one side. "You don't mean that you…? That you are…?"

"The one and only," Cyrus replied coldly, though

he could admit there was a certain satisfaction that, at last, she knew him.

"But you had a different name. You were not called *Cyrus Ashkan*. You were known instead as—"

"I am, according to some, Justin Arthur Cyrus George. Then a viscount. Now an earl, or so I am told."

She was already nodding along, looking more animated than she had since he'd stormed down that aisle in an Italian church and removed her from that wedding that should never have taken place.

"Viscount Highborough," Hope breathed. "Earl Alcott. I know that story. Everyone knows that story." But she seemed to think she should tell it to the person who knew it best, sitting up and leaning forward. "Your mother was one of the great supermodels of her time and also happened to be from the British aristocracy. Her face was everywhere—until she met your father at some event and they fell madly and instantly in love. He swept her off into his desert kingdom, and everyone expected them to live happily ever after. But they didn't. She only stayed there for a little while. A year? Two?"

"Five," Cyrus corrected her softly.

"And then, when they were back in England visiting her family, she ran off with the King's baby." Hope blinked, presumably because she recalled who she was speaking to. "You."

"Me," he agreed.

"I don't really know what happened then. But it was years, wasn't it?"

"I was four," Cyrus told her, his voice as even as he could make it, though he could not imagine why revisiting these memories should affect him. Why those old songs should move in him again, when he would have told himself he'd long since forgot the melodies. "For the first year after my mother left him, running off under cover of night, my father attempted to fight her out in the open. But she came from a very old family. She was the only child of the old Earl and thanks to him, there was no relief to be found in an English court."

"What did he do?"

"He waited. Because what my mother did not understand is that the people of the desert do not recognize time. There is only sand. Sun. And stone that is slowly and inexorably washed away by the exposure. I was twelve when my father and his men liberated me from captivity."

"That's not quite how I heard the story told," she said, and Cyrus could not place her tone. It sounded almost… But no. Who would pity a king? "They kidnapped you. It became an international incident."

"There were those who wished for to become such a thing, yes," Cyrus agreed. "But it is one thing to sit in the concrete streets of London and declare this or that to stir up the British populace. It is something else again to find one's way through the treacherous Aminabad sands. No one managed to do so. My father kept me hidden for six more years so that my mother could enjoy being without her child the way that he had been forced to do."

"That sounds difficult." But there was something about the way she said that, as if her sympathies were not where they should have been.

"It was just," he told her. "And when I was of age, I could do as I pleased without worrying about being kidnapped by my mother. I returned to that cold island so that I too could enjoy this education that men must have to convince other, lesser men that they are equals."

"I saw a documentary about it," she said quietly. "Your mother's position is that your father poisoned you against her."

"She is the poison," Cyrus retorted, mildly enough. "As I told her myself before I started university in England, the better to disabuse her of any fantasies that we might enjoy some sort of reunion. But as long as she poisons only herself with it, what should I care? I know the truth of things. But my mother's deficiencies are not the point of telling this tale, Hope. I require neither your sympathy nor your concern."

"Noted," she said, but her expression was nothing but smooth when he frowned at her.

He pushed on. "While I was at Oxford, my father and I agreed that it would be a work of strategic importance to put to rest, once and for all, the notion that my father's quarrel with my mother was my country's quarrel with England."

"That makes sense." She shrugged, and he thought her deeply unserious, which he would have told her if he'd imagined she'd take it as the insult it was. But she was too languid, waving that hand as she did. "Nobody likes a quarrel."

He should not have found her fascinating, quite against his will. It would have been easier to shrug off the promises he had made. He had considered doing it many times in the years since her father had died, given her seeming disinterest in the promises that bound them together.

But breaking promises was something soft, weak, poisonous creatures like his mother did, claiming it was a virtue. Claiming she was saving them both, Cyrus and her, long ago.

Cyrus had made himself a man who did not make promises he did not keep.

No matter what.

"I could see the wisdom in the strategy," Cyrus said reprovingly now. "Given the legal skirmishes my parents had engaged in when I was younger. And so my father's mother—also an Englishwoman, as is tradition—approached your father and the two of them came to an agreement. This has always been our way."

"This promise you say he made." Hope shook her head. "I told you, I don't know anything about it. And even if I did, he's gone. I wish he wasn't, but one thing I've learned is that wishes do not come true."

"We are not speaking of wishes," Cyrus told her with a certain quiet ruthlessness.

If his tone troubled her, she did not show it. "And I know they don't come true, because I've tried. Again and again and again."

There was something in the way she said that. It made its way beneath his skin when he should have been immune.

Perhaps that was why he sounded so severe when he continued. "It is not a wish, but a fact, that your father promised your hand to me on your eighteenth birthday.

Or, if you took it upon yourself to go to university to educate yourself, upon your graduation."

She made a soft little sound. "He didn't. He wouldn't. Would he?"

"He did. And yet you were walking down that aisle to marry another man." He found he was leaning forward himself now, his gaze so intent on hers it almost felt as if this was a kiss. *Almost.* "Quite as if no promises had ever been made at all."

CHAPTER THREE

THIS WAS BEGINNING to feel like a bit of a roller coaster and Hope had never been any kind of fan of amusement park rides. She didn't even like a too-fast car, much less the games some liked to play on small watercraft.

No, thank you. She liked her stomach to stay put.

But that didn't appear to be an option available to her today.

Not when the most beautiful man she'd ever encountered had not only snatched her out of the jaws of her own wedding, but claimed she'd been promised to him, too. Wholly unbeknownst to her.

"That seems a bit harsh," she pointed out, while her stomach put on a little bit of a show inside her. She would have told herself she was hungry, that was all, had she not stuffed herself. This was…a different sort of hunger.

"Does it?" Cyrus sounded wholly unrepentant, his midnight eyes dark. "I would have said that the breaking of promises was far harsher than any discussion of them. But I am an elemental creature, as you will soon discover."

Hope thought she was doing pretty well, trying her best to make sense of what was meant to be her step forward into the role of wife to a stranger that had taken a dramatic left turn into the clutches of Cyrus Ashkan, a man who had been his own soap opera, back in the day. Who hadn't pored over every article? Every picture? Every questionable tell-all from supposed staff?

Her own story paled in comparison to his. First she'd been frog-marched from car to helicopter, helicopter to plane. Then she'd been…fed, which did not seem to fit with the frog-marching. Then he'd told her the story of his own infamous kidnapping, though he didn't seem to view it the way the rest of the world did. *He* did not seem to mind that no one had laid eyes on the boy Cyrus had been for all of those years. *He* appeared to be under the impression that his mother was the villain.

His mother, who had never modeled again, had been seen in public only when petitioning various members of the government to take up her cause, and who had been considered a study in parental grief ever after.

Especially once Cyrus had reappeared and had been nothing short of scathing toward her and about her.

But all of that, as sensational as it was, paled in comparison to the notion that her beloved father had married her off to some stranger long ago, then had never mentioned it again… Though, of course, he had intended to live.

He would have thought he had time.

Oh, how she wished he'd had time—

Hope decided she couldn't possibly think too much

about that part of it. Not now. Not yet. Not until she knew what she was in for.

Hope was inclined to wonder if this was all some kind of pre-wedding dream she was having, trying to save herself at the last minute from a marriage that was certainly better than the kinds she'd assumed she'd likely have to suffer. But still wasn't exactly what she would call *desirable.*

After all, while Lionel Asensio had many fine qualities—mostly that he wished for her to play a very specific marital role for his family with very clear requirements, none of which were icky—it was not as if, deep down, Hope had *wanted* to marry him.

She wasn't thrilled about *this* turn of events either, no matter how good the food was. What didn't track was the way this man was looking at her as if she, personally, had made him promises. And then had recklessly and thoughtlessly and deliberately broken them.

It was almost funny. Truly, she almost laughed, because if she'd had the faintest notion that there was someone she could have run to she would have done it ages ago.

But Cyrus Ashkan was far too *elemental* to appreciate a bit of helpless laughter, she was betting. Particularly if it was at his own expense.

"If you believe that I betrayed you, then I don't understand why you would go to the trouble of ruining my wedding today," she pointed out. Very reasonably, to her mind. "You're well shot of me, I would have thought."

"This is your response?" He looked relaxed in the seat across from her, though that fire in his dark gaze told a different tale. “This is another inappropriate attempt at humor, I can only assume. Do you believe that this kind of defiance will be tolerated?”

“Until about ten minutes ago, I didn’t even know who you were,” she reminded him, gently enough. “I haven’t given a lot of thought to what it is you will or won’t tolerate.” She shrugged—partially because the last time she had done it, his eyes had widened. As if he’d never seen such a thing in all his days. “Anyway, I can’t be responsible for a promise or a contract or a handshake I didn’t know anything about. My father never mentioned it or you. So, I’m sorry? I guess?”

And there was something about the way he stared at her then. Some level of unholy fury though he sat perfectly still.

Too still, something in her whispered.

As if his was the stillness of a great predator, a scant moment before it attacked. All that focus. All that *intensity.* And the scope of what was about to happen already visible in that dark gaze, if she dared look close enough—

Hope found herself holding her breath, wanting things she could not name, but he did not come for her.

Not then.

She told herself she was relieved, not disappointed, when instead he rose from his seat. Then stepped away, moving toward the back of the plane to speak in a language she didn’t understand with his ever-watchful men.

The men she could admit she’d forgotten were even here.

Hope assured herself that her stomach was *fine*, not

madly flipping this way or that *at all*, and settled further into her seat. Because she still couldn't think what, exactly, she should do otherwise. Despite the amount of action films she'd watched in her time, she doubted very much that a person who didn't have the slightest idea how a plane worked could land one.

And Hope needed to make sure she did not crash, nor get too caught up in the palm of Cyrus's hand or whatever he'd been going on about, because she still needed to save her mother.

As always, there was that…grief and helpless adoration inside her every time she thought about Mignon. Every time she thought about the past few years and how she'd been so sure her wedding would make it so they were both happy again—

But then, maybe that was why she wasn't reacting to this abduction the way she should have been. The way anyone else would have been, surely. This was the first time since her father had died that Hope could say, with complete honesty, that there was absolutely nothing she could do to solve this or fix this or make it better.

She couldn't *work harder* and come up with any sort of solution here. She couldn't *think out of the box* and make something happen. There was nothing to *do*. Sooner or later the plane would land. And maybe then she would feel slightly less relieved than she did now. Maybe she would feel fear. Or the stirrings of temper to paper it over. Maybe then she would once again take up the great worry she always usually felt about Mignon.

Maybe then she would ask herself how, precisely,

this controlling man would let her care for her mother when he famously liked his own so little.

But her stomach was pleasantly full, no matter how he might have looked at her like a great big *thing* about to pounce. And the drone of the plane's engines was like white noise, lulling her as she sat there, letting the adrenaline drain right out of her.

And for once, there was literally nothing she could do for her mother except love her as she always did.

She would have to come up with something a bit more concrete once they landed.

Her eyelids grew heavier and heavier, or maybe it was that she could hear Cyrus's raspy growl of a voice from the back of the plane, so commanding, so intense, even using words she couldn't comprehend.

Either way, before she knew it, she had fallen asleep.

And then came awake again in a jolting hurry some time later—

Only to realize that it wasn't really *jolting*, it was the plane bumping along a deserted runway as it came in for a landing. Controlled jolting, anyway.

Hope was aware of too many things at once. The light, pouring in through the plane's windows, so much brighter and hotter than anything she'd ever seen. She squinted out the windows to get a sense of where she was, but there was…nothing.

At first she thought it was an optical illusion, but then she realized. This was the desert. The blue sky above, the endless, undulating sand like some kind of sea, and nothing else.

In all directions, that same *nothing.*

And then there was Cyrus besides, standing in the aisle above her seat and looking at her with an expression she could not pretend to read.

"Oh," Hope murmured, scrubbing at her face with the heels of her hands. "I guess I fell asleep. That tracks. I haven't been doing much of that lately either."

"None of that matters," he intoned from on high.

Hope found herself sitting up a bit straighter, though she couldn't have said why she thought *her posture* would help here. It was something about the way he looked down the length of his body at her, as if looking down from some immense altar. Or mountaintop.

Or some impossible desert sky.

"It matters to me," she pointed out, because she couldn't seem to help herself. "The importance of good sleep habits can't be exaggerated, Cyrus."

"We have landed on Aminabad soil," he told her, and again, there was a certain cadence to the way he spoke. As if he was issuing proclamations. It was notably different from the way he had been speaking to her before. This was not…*speaking.* This was not *a conversation.* She understood that instinctively. "Allow me to welcome you to your new life, Hope Cartwright. *Hayati. Rohi. Omri.*" He intoned those words in such a way that she knew at once that they were endearments—and more, that he was making certain she heard the ironic way he was saying them. "You have been honored immeasurably, little though you deserve it, and are become my wife."

She wanted to laugh. But she couldn't, quite.

Not quite.

It all felt too fraught, somehow.

There was something in the way he studied her, with a suppressed sort of intensity—though she could see the gleam of it clearly enough, there in his dark gaze. She could see the way he held himself too still once more. She could feel the difference in the air between them. And there was something, too, in the way her body responded to that difference. It was as if she'd been plunged into a cold pool and was even now standing at the edge, shivering.

God—was she actually *shivering*?

Hope made herself stand up, though that put her perilously close to him. Too close, by far, to this intense and compelling stranger who spoke of promises broken. Of her as his wife, of all things.

Now that the plane had landed and there was nothing outside that she could see in any direction, save an endless expanse of waiting desert, she found she possessed far less equanimity than she'd felt in the air. When all she'd been able to concentrate on was the fact that she was not even now married to Lionel Asensio.

She couldn't really access the wild relief she'd felt then any longer. Mostly because, if she wasn't married to Lionel, that meant she still needed to sort out a way to take care of her mother. And herself.

At the same time, she didn't want Cyrus to know that. Not really. She didn't want him to guess that she didn't feel the same way she had since he'd swooped in and rescued her—and who cared how or why he'd come to do that? He'd done it all the same.

She would prefer it if he continued to think she was relatively unaffected by all of this.

Hope opted not to question herself on that.

"Did I sleep through our wedding?" she asked instead, aiming for the dry, amused tone that had come so naturally to her before. "I feel certain I would have woken up for a whole wedding ceremony. Given I'm already dressed for it."

Something she would not call a smile moved over his hard face and echoed inside her like a tuning fork. "There is no need for a wedding ceremony, *omri*. My word is law."

He stepped back then, and curtly indicated that she should step past him to walk toward the blazing light that it took her long, stupid moments to realize was the door to the outside. Hope cleared her throat and told herself it was the desert air that was even now drying out sinuses that had been born and bred in England's greenest, most humid hills.

It didn't occur to her not to obey him. She had not the faintest shred of a defiant thought. And when she realized that, she rationalized it away. Because what did she plan to do instead? Stage a sit-in on the plane? She'd bet that would end pretty quickly once they turned off the air-conditioning and she began to broil.

There was nothing for it but to march outside into all that blinding light, so that was what Hope did.

Because that was what she always did.

No matter how overwhelming a thing looked, she charged straight for it, because the only thing worse than an overwhelming thing was dreading it.

She made her way down the jet's stairs, finding her darling wedding slippers a rather poor match for the tarmac. And the whole *desert* situation. There was sand swirling this way and that every time the faint and inconstant breeze felt like moving it along. The heat was oppressive. It seemed to *glow* into her. It wasn't like a face full of sunshine. It was like the heat started *within her* and was setting her alight from the inside out.

Hope felt as if she was burning alive already and she hadn't even had time to sweat.

She felt Cyrus come down the stairs behind her, then stop—close enough that she had the panicked notion that she could actually differentiate desert heat all around her from the heat he gave off, and both heat sources were far too much for her—

Though thinking things like that could not possibly help her here.

The plane's door folded back in on itself and the plane began to move again, bumping slowly along the tarmac at first, then picking up speed. Then, too quickly for Hope's taste, hurtling itself off into the cloudless sky that seemed to press down upon them like a great blue fist.

She watched the plane fly away until it was a small dot on the horizon and her eyes hurt from the glare.

Or possibly also because she was trying her very best to keep tears at bay. When she never cried. Not since the night her father had died—because what was the point? It didn't bring him back. It didn't change a thing.

Still, that felt a lot like the wrong question to ask herself just now. Here on a rapidly disappearing tarmac, surrounded by shifting sand on all sides.

And the man who called himself *lord* of this alien place.

She didn't look at him. Not yet. She scoured the horizon instead, desperate to find something that whispered of civilization *somewhere.*

But there was nothing.

The endless, pitiless blue sky above. White sands in every direction, rising and falling like hills. Like waves.

Like the end of her, something in her whispered.

Yet that whisper didn't feel *too much.* It felt something much more like *right.*

Which might have been the most frightening thing of all, had she allowed herself to focus on it.

"Beautiful, is it not?" Cyrus intoned in that way of his, as if he was proclaiming it to the skies and sand. Imprinting them with his will.

"I can see how someone might find it beautiful," Hope hedged. Her lips were already dry and she truly couldn't tell if that was the desert air or her own mounting panic. "It's not what I'm used to, I can tell you that. So much sky. And all that *sand.* One expects a desert to be *sandy*, of course, but I still feel entirely unprepared for the *immensity—*"

She realized she was babbling and stopped herself in the next moment.

Even though it made her throat hurt.

She pressed her tongue against the roof of her mouth, hard, and made herself turn to face Cyrus. To squint at him through all this *light.* So much light that the glare of it felt like another source of heat, all on its own and apart from the temperature, scalding her eyes in their sockets.

That seemed as good a reason to feel faintly teary as any.

And looking at the man before her was not *soothing*, exactly. Nothing about him was *soothing*. He was his own immensity. He stood there, a dark slash of color against all that blue and white. His gaze was near black. His face seemed even more bronze, set against the landscape that pressed in on all sides.

He merely regarded her as if she was the curiosity here. As if she didn't fit, and she believed it. Because even though he wore a suit, she could tell that he belonged right here in this overwhelming place. That the desert had made him, no matter how many years he'd spent in England.

That he was made of the lonely sands, rolling on forever. That he was too expansive to fit beneath the gray clouds of England, the manicured fields, the old stone walls cutting the land into digestible parcels for too many centuries to count.

He looked like the desert, she thought, and then felt herself flush. Because she was being fanciful and that wasn't like her at all.

"I think I'm dehydrating as we speak," she told him, attempting to sound something close enough to cheerful. "In another moment I'll be a crumbling husk and the breeze will scatter me all over this tarmac until I'm indistinguishable from the sand."

For a moment Cyrus did not respond, and she thought

he wouldn't. That he would stand here and watch as she blew away before him like dust.

"I do not expect you to appreciate the desert," he told her, and though his tone was bland enough she could see the faint disapproval all over him. A different sort of disapproval than the kind he'd been aiming at her since they'd met. This was less about vague promises he'd claimed had been made and more about *her*. What he clearly saw as the deficiencies in her character, immediately evident in the fact that she was not *instantly in love* with this stark, terrifyingly empty place. "I expected nothing else."

"Did you love it at first sight?" she dared to toss right back at him. Maybe it really was the dehydration setting in and collapse was imminent. "When you found yourself here again as a twelve-year-old, was your first reaction *joy*?"

His face seemed to harden, becoming more a part of that glare. "My first and only reaction was gratitude that my father saw fit to return me to myself."

"Really. Not even the briefest moment—"

"But you will have ample time to get used to the sky and the sand," he continued, something cutting and ruthless in the way he said it. "As you will never leave this desert again."

That was clearly meant to land like a blow. And maybe it would have, if Hope had been anyone else.

But she had taken far too many blows in her time. Too many to even bother counting. This one didn't even feel like a blow. It was more like a kiss—

Not that she wanted to think about *kissing* when this close to him. In all his…*state.*

She didn't *quite* laugh, squinting off toward one or other impossible horizon. "*Never* is a long time."

"I told you. You are become my wife, Hope."

Hope opened her mouth to argue that point, but stopped herself. Because the *way* he kept saying that finally registered. It was…almost archaic, really.

Like another proclamation.

Like a law might sound in a place like this.

She was too hot to *shiver*, surely. "You keep saying that."

"I am anxious for you to hear me, Hope."

Yet she could not make herself believe, for so much as an instant, that this man was anxious about anything, nor ever had been. "I hear you. But I don't understand."

"This is the Aminabad Desert and I am its lord," he told her, a certain satisfaction in his tone. In his gaze. All over him, in fact. "What I declare becomes fact, and then is made law. That is the way of things here." When she only squinted back at him, he relented. Slightly. "If I say you are my wife, we are married. It is done."

Hope still thought she might topple over—and would have, probably, if she didn't think she'd sizzle like a proper English fry-up right there on the tarmac, and her here without a hangover that needed that kind of indulgent mopping up—but sighed instead.

"Felicitations to us both, then. I guess?" She found her hands on her hips, somehow. "I think you'd better tell me what that means to you, Cyrus."

Was that the first time she'd said his actual name? It

felt illicit. Like stolen chocolate, melting on her tongue. She was sure she could feel the way his eyes blazed. As sure as she was that he felt it too, that melting.

Heatstroke, she told herself. That was all.

His dark brows arched high, command and condemnation at once, and no sign whatever of any reaction to the heat. "I don't actually know you. I don't know what you want in a wife. I don't know your feelings about marriage at all, much less what it means in a cultural sense in a country I've never visited before."

Hope really did laugh then, because it was that or give herself over to the heat. Her dry lips. That urge to cry, collapse, or both. That terrifying *melting* that felt worse than all of those combined.

She hurried on. "This might come as a shock to you, but I am something of an expert when it comes to various takes on the institution of marriage. I've discussed it at length, with all manner of people, and I can tell you that none of them agree. On anything, really. So when you tell me, in all your state, that I am *become your wife*—you're going to have to tell me what you mean by that. In detail, so there can be no mistake."

"You have already made the last mistake you will make," Cyrus told her, his voice a low and dangerous thread that she could hear all too well above the breeze. Above the sound of her own heart, pounding much too hard. "Your indifference to the promises made in your name has showed me your character, but I have chosen to marry you anyway. In time, I am certain you will thank me for this gift."

"Why would you *gift* someone you hated on sight?"

Hope asked, and that was when the laughter she'd been holding at bay—possibly because it was a touch hysterical—bubbled up. "Surely it would have been easier to leave me to it. I certainly wouldn't have known any different."

"But I would have. And regardless of what you do or do not do, *I* keep my promises."

"That doesn't sound like much of a foundation for a marriage," she managed to say, not laughing any longer.

"And what was the foundation for the marriage you intended to embark upon today?" he asked, his brows high and his dark gaze intent on hers. "You could not wait to tell me it was no love match. That you were as happy to marry him, or me, as any other. By your own rationale, why should you care why I have chosen to elevate you in this manner?"

She wanted to tell him she didn't care. She wanted to sweep everything he'd said aside and focus on the things she did care about, like making sure her mother was cared for. She wanted to defend herself, though she wasn't even sure what accusations he was making—because he was right. Wasn't he? Why should she care who she married?

The again, she'd never encountered a man who got beneath her skin like this.

And maybe it was the heat. Maybe it was sunstroke. But she had the strangest, fairy-tale-like notion that it was possible she did the same to him.

That maybe, just maybe, she wasn't the only one feeling all this. That if she dared reach over and put her hand on his chest, his heart would roar as hers did.

"Fair enough," she whispered.

He nodded, as if it was done. As if they were set in stone now, her and him. That, too, should have terrified her. "There is nothing left to you now but a life of quiet obedience, locked away from the world as if you were never here at all."

"You say that like it's a punishment," she managed to say, even producing a slightly less hysterical little laugh. "But it sounds like a holiday."

"It will be no holiday." There, before her, he seemed to grow in size. He was an immensity on par with the desert that surrounded them. His dark eyes flashed, the darkest midnight she had ever beheld. "It will be an exercise in humility."

"Cyrus..." she murmured, not certain what she wished to say to him. What she *could* say.

"I kept waiting for you to remember yourself," he told her. "To remember that you were promised to one who waited for you to come to him, but this never occurred. Right up to this farce of a wedding, which you should have known I would never allow to take place."

Hope could only listen to this in a kind of awe. Aware, on some level, that deep inside there was a trembling. Maybe even a yearning—to imagine that someone, anyone, had looked out for her these last years.

Though perhaps that was temper, not longing, that he had watched her over these past years and failed to intervene. Either way, she was completely unable to tear her gaze from his.

"It is lucky for you that you appeal to me, *omri*," he told her, and the strangest thing was that she really did feel lucky for a long, dizzying sort of moment. Then he kept talking. "I did not expect that you would, but I am happy to accept the gift of your body in return for the mercy I have shown you already, and the incalculable honor I bestow upon you by marrying you."

"Will my body truly be a gift in this marriage of yours?" She made herself ask the question, somehow not giving in to the trembling thing deep inside her that she was terribly afraid was not fear at all, but desire. Another thing she had never felt before. "Will it be mine to give—or not give? Notably unlike this kidnap?"

"You will beg to bestow this gift of yours upon me," he assured her, as if he knew. As if he could see the future. And the look on his face was so intense that she thought for a moment that she could see it too. Because the mad whirl deep inside her was unlike anything she had ever felt before in her life. Almost as if it really was a gift, these things he thundered at her so sternly in all this wild heat. "But you may be certain that I will never give you the gift of my sons."

Hope blinked at that, and maybe it was a welcome break from all those vast things inside her, changing her where she stood. "No gifts in the form of sons I didn't ask for. Got it."

Cyrus took a step closer, making her catch her breath. Then he reached out and took her chin between his fingers.

That was all. A minor touch, really. Nothing at all in the grand scheme of things.

But she could feel the strength of him, the heat. She knew without having to ask that he was a man who took pride in the fact he used his own hands. There was nothing soft on him. The was not so much as the faintest hint.

"I will enslave you with passion," he informed her, and even though the way he said that was almost remote, the look in his gaze was nothing short of a forest fire. And here in a place where there were no trees, the only thing that could burn was her. "There are few women on this earth who can resist the Supreme Ruler of the Great Sands, and I doubt very much you are one of them."

"Thanks for that," Hope managed to reply, though she felt dizzy again. And *on fire*. "That's something to look forward to, then. Supreme and sandy passion on command."

"I will use you and then cast you aside," he told her, almost tenderly. A new promise. "I will sentence you to a life of fruitless yearning in my harem, a drudge of a wife with no standing while the other wives I will marry give me many, many sons. This is the life you have earned, and you will thank me for it."

She heard him. On some level, she even understood what he was saying. Drudgery, yearning, unlikely expressions of gratitude on her end. But his hand was on her chin, his fingers pressing into her flesh. And all she could seem to do was tip her head back and gaze up at him, as if he really was as powerful as the desert sun.

Maybe more.

"R-right," she managed to stammer out. "Used and cast aside, no standing. With the passion."

It was the passion as punishment part she couldn't really get past.

The part that made something deeply feminine and knowing, tucked away in a place she'd never encountered within herself before, turn over and stretch. Like it was waking up after a long sleep.

Like it had been waiting there, just beyond desire, all the while.

But there was no time to worry about such things, *knowing* or passion or the kind of punishment that Cyrus still seemed to think sounded like something other than a luxury retreat. There was no time left.

He dropped his fingers from her chin. He raised his arm, up over his head in a grand sort of slashing motion, as if he meant to slice the sky above in two.

Bringing with it a pack of horses from behind the hills, descending upon them like riders on a storm.

Like fate.

And there was a part of her that was rightly overwhelmed. More than overwhelmed, as Cyrus swung her up into the saddle of a horse, then held her up in front of him, like the spoils of war.

But inside, in that part of her that was newly awake, she was smiling.

CHAPTER FOUR

CYRUS RODE AT the head of the pack of fine Aminabad horses, as befit him as the Lord and King.

And he was not certain he had ever felt more like a desert king of yore than he did now. The merciless sun above, the sand below. His men at his back and a woman caught up before him, in that great white dress that billowed around them as his cavalry galloped with him over the dunes.

It was almost enough to make him wish his father was still alive, that the old man might see that he had achieved what he had always set out to achieve. He had made his only son over into an appropriate heir to this ancient, dusty kingdom, despite the best attempts of the mother who had stolen Cyrus away.

Yet as he rode, he found that he thought less of what he must do as King and more of the needs that rose in him—as a man. Because he had claimed this woman as his wife. Not merely some bit of sweet flesh for an evening's entertainment. And she sat before him, as wives and captives alike had done for centuries on horses like his, the lush curves of her bottom nestled up tight against his sex.

Making sure that ache in him only grew as the miles passed.

An ache he intended that she would soothe, though he had not lied to her. He wanted her, yes. That wanting had astonished and outraged him—that was also true.

But he wanted her to give herself to him, this woman who would marry another so cold-bloodedly.

He wanted her wild with wanting him.

She was fair, which would do her no good in the desert heat. And so he had taken the time to wrap scarves around her as they'd started their ride, covering her hair and the skin that already looked flushed from the sun's merciless rays.

But even though he knew those scarves protected her, he resented them.

For he could not see that delectable curve of her chin. Or the way she held her mouth, giving herself away in a thousand different small expressions he was not certain she even knew she made.

Yet he did. He knew far too much after an afternoon's observation of her. In person.

He could have headed to the south, where the heart of his country's wealth was arrayed around the oil fields that brought in the Western businessmen to try their wheeling and dealing and imagine they were cannier than the tribe who had been living off the bounty of this desert forever. There in the southern oases lay the commercial center of his country. The marketplaces, the businesses, and the many dwellings of those in his tribe who did not wish to follow the seasons north and south the way their ancestors had. He supposed they were cities, in truth, though he did not like that word.

But in any case, that was not where he was headed. He turned to the north instead, and made haste across the shifting sands for the fortress that had once been all that protected his people from their enemies.

He meant for it to do so again.

They rode hard, for the sands seemed restless today, and wise men never tested the will of the sands. They knew too well that if they did, they would lose—and usually more than any one man could bear.

It was a solid hour's ride, flat out, from the northern tarmac they only used regularly. For it was too easily swallowed whole by the dunes and was often lost, no matter how many men were dispatched to keep it clear.

The sands did ever as they wished.

That was one of the first things Cyrus had learned when his father's men had brought him here.

Today, like then, he saw the fortress first. He only rode faster at the sight, but he still knew the very moment that the woman in his arms saw it too. He felt something like an electric shock go through her body and he thought she might say something, but she did not.

And he wondered if she was having the same experience that he'd had as that twelve-year-old boy who had barely remembered the desert from his youth. His father had expected that. He had anticipated and had brought Cyrus here for the same reasons that Cyrus was bringing Hope here today.

Because there was nothing like a medieval fortress,

plunked down in the middle of an inhospitable desert stretching out to the horizon on all sides, to encourage a person to get right with themselves. And the desert itself.

Though as a child, what he had felt was…overwhelmed.

His father had seemed cruel to him then, overbearing and ferocious, and he missed the mother he'd loved, then.

These things seemed impossible to him now, but riding up to the fortress again, like this, brought it all back.

First, Cyrus remembered, he hadn't believed what he saw before him. He'd been certain that he'd gotten something in his eyes at first—presumably sand. That would explain the smudge he saw, off the distance.

The closer they got, the more he had blinked and blinked, because there was nothing. There was nothing but the dance of the sand, the whisper of the wind, the movement of the horse beneath him. And only the endless, cloudless sky above.

As a twelve-year-old boy, he hadn't known how to explain to himself what was happening. Why his mind kept filling in the vast expanses when there was only desert—until he'd realized that he couldn't blink what he was seeing away. That it was a great wall rising from the desert floor—and they were riding straight for it.

That the cruel man who had taken him from his home and hauled him here intended to keep him in what had looked, to him, like a prison.

When you found yourself here again as a twelve-year-old, was your first reaction joy? Hope had asked him.

Inexplicably, he heard his mother's singing in his head once more.

And before him, he could feel the way Hope shook his grip, and more, how she fought to repress it.

He knew exactly what battle she was fighting.

And he told himself that he was glad. That he should congratulate himself, for this was all going precisely as planned. She was his now, as had been promised long ago. He had kept his vows.

Now all that remained was making sure she regretted what she'd done while he'd been waiting for her to take her place at his side.

The pack of horses, Cyrus at the front and twelve of his men arrayed around him, rode toward the steep, forbidding walls of the fortress and did not slow their steeds as they approached.

He felt the woman—his wife, he reminded himself again, for so had he decreed—brace herself as it seemed they might dash themselves against the very rocks that rose before them.

Instead, at the last moment, his men let out a cry. It was answered high up on the battlements and thus the great gate was raised.

They thundered straight through, coming to a stop in the grand court.

Cyrus took a moment to remind himself that he, too, had once looked around this place with awe and wonder, so different was it from the ruins of English castles and the like that he had known while in his mother's possession.

Different, though its tactical uses were much the

same. Like any fortress, it was built as much to keep people within as to keep marauders without.

He rather thought that was the part Hope was wrestling with as she looked around, golden eyes wide from behind her scarves. For all the ornate scrollwork, tile and mosaic and flourishes, fountains and hints of greenery on the other side of the archways, this was to be her prison, just as it had once been his.

Perhaps she was perceptive enough to know it.

And perhaps it would even be the making of her, as it had once been for him.

He slung his leg over and dismounted his favorite horse, then took his woman down after him, letting her body brush against his as he lowered her feet to the earth.

His woman. His earth.

And once again, he could feel that blazing thing between them, as much an insult as it was intriguing.

Cyrus had not anticipated that he would want her like this.

That he could *make* her want him, he had not doubted at all. Feminine eyes followed him wherever he went, whether here in the desert or out there in the wider world. They did not even need to know who he was to gaze hungrily at him wherever he went.

He had seen a similar hunger in her gaze, too, and had every intention of using it against her—of doing exactly what he'd told her he would, making her into nothing more than a mindless, careless slave to sensation. His to command.

Cyrus would build that fire in her, then let her burn out the rest of her days.

This had always been his intention, because it would keep the promise he had made but also incorporate the punishment he felt she deserved for ignoring her part of the bargain struck for her. But it was not until now, surrounded by his men on all sides, the thick walls of the grand fortress rising all around them, that he fully understood that he would enjoy it too.

Far more than he had anticipated he might when he had only watched her from afar.

He sensed more than heard her sharp intake of breath, but even as he did he stepped back to put space between them. Because he did not enjoy parading his private life about in front of the world. He'd had his fill of such things when he was a child.

Instead, Cyrus glanced to one side, where his man of arms waited and raised his brow. His man nodded, and that was all the communication necessary. Cyrus knew that everything was as he had asked. That while he had flown off to Italy to handle this situation before it got even worse, his people had handled things here in this usually abandoned place in accordance with his wishes.

"I would not have you in this gown," he told Hope then, looking back at her with some small measure of pity as he imagined, in detail, what awaited her. What he would demand of her. "This gown you wore when you imagined you would marry another man."

"It's less comfortable than you might imagine," she said in that way she had, as if she imagined she was being helpful in some way. Because apparently, she did not have it within her to feel even the slightest hint of the shame she ought to have felt at her own behavior. She even smiled, confounding him. “But, fun fact about being carried off from your own wedding ceremony—I don’t have anything else to wear.”

“That will not be an issue,” he told her. In repressive tones that, as usual, appeared to have no effect on this woman.

It made him wonder what would.

He raised a hand then, and the women came. They spilled out from inside the fortress’s mosaiced walls and came hurrying toward him. Once there, they fanned out around Hope, sneaking glances her way while they kept their gazes lowered before their king.

“The women will ready you,” he told his wife.

His wife.

Grandly, he could admit.

But she did not look cowed like the rest. Though she did not look quite as relaxed as she had on the plane, either. He chose to take that as some kind of victory.

“Dare I ask what I am to be ready for?” she asked.

“I’m sure they will prepare you sufficiently.” He waved his hand at the women around her. “I believe they have perhaps seven English words between them, should you imagine you can sway them to your side. Their job is to make you acceptable. To make certain that their king is not offended by you in any way.”

“Too late,” Hope murmured.

He ignored that. “Your job is to submit to their ministrations, no matter how odd they may seem to you.”

"Thank you." Her voice was dry, her golden gaze sharp. "That's very comforting."

"Did I not make myself clear? It is not my aim to make you comfortable, Hope, *omri*. That will never be a goal of mine."

He thought she might wilt at that. Anyone would. But instead, *this* woman smiled at him. A great, big, brilliant sort of smile that made him grind his teeth together. Because she shouldn't flash that around. It should come with a warning, that smile. Particularly in a place like this, where it could only reflect the sky and the sun, and she risked blinding the whole kingdom.

But he did not wish to tell her such things, so he settled for a scowl instead.

And then made himself turn away and stride off when what he wanted was to watch her go—an urge he could make no sense of.

But as the afternoon wore on, he found it was far more difficult to lose himself in the usual matters of state than expected. This fortress was set up to withstand modern as well as medieval attacks, and thus had been renovated in his father's time so that it could function as a reasonable office if necessary.

It is necessary, his father had told him years ago, when he was at the end of his reign. Cyrus had come back from his years in England by then, filled with sheer delight to be out of all that rain. *You and I might wish that this place could remain untouched by the march of time, but wishes only highlight our weaknesses, my son. We must use them only as guides toward what we should eradicate.*

Cyrus found himself repeating those words again and again as the day wore on.

Because he knew exactly what the female attendants were doing with Hope. They knew nothing of any rumors about her. What should they care about what happened in far-off lands? They knew her only as their king's new bride. As the Lord's first wife.

First they would have swept her off into the old harem that he'd ordered aired out and redone to his specifications. These days, the Lord of the Aminabad Desert did not live in a palace that was easily discoverable from above in a time of satellite imagery. He did not gather all his people's valuables into one place, inviting attack.

Cyrus preferred to make himself more difficult to be found.

He had turned the country's ancient Royal Palace into a set of museums, so that his people could enjoy the spoils of their own wealth as they pleased. He himself split his time between different compounds, not because he was paranoid like his father, but because his tribe had always been nomadic.

And Cyrus found his people loved him all the more when he made himself accessible to them in the old ways, moving from place to place and speaking with those he asked to follow him. So that every citizen and every region might consider themselves as royal as the next.

But this fortress was something else again. It had been built in a different time. When the King was a warlord and one of the greatest sources of his wealth and consequence was the women he collected and the sons they gave him.

As a child, he had explored the old harem himself. He'd wandered in and out of the alcove rooms gathered around the central courtyard, with its grand fountain in the middle, pools for all, trees and flowers and every detail carefully thought out to proclaim the glory of the desert Lord. So that even when the women were not tending to their master's needs in the royal bed, they might think of him. Long for him.

Vie for his favor.

It was there, in the baths that were fed by the warm spring deep beneath the fortress, that the women would be tending to the undeserving woman he had elevated to the coveted position as his first wife, because that was the promise he had made long ago. They would take that wedding dress, meant for another man, and burn it. They would cover Hope in oil, massaging it into her skin. They would make certain that all blemishes and unsightly hairs were covered or removed, according to his preferences and the custom of the land.

And they would tell her that was what they were doing, whether they used English words for that or not, so that she would know at every moment that everything that was happening to her was to make her his.

Entirely his.

Only once they had tended to the standards of beauty that he required would they bathe her, washing every part of her and allowing no modesty. They would lather her once with handcrafted soaps, then again with sweet sand, then a third time with scented lotions, moving her from pool to pool until she was clean. Ready. Only then would they anoint her.

This time, when they applied oils, it would be to make her glow. To make her hair gleam. To make her skin soft and supple.

They would bedeck her in jewels as befitted the wife of their lord. Then they would drape her in silks and perfume her all over before, at last, they brought her to him.

He knew this was a process. That it would take the time it took.

And still Cyrus found himself counting the minutes. As if he were little more than the adolescent he had been when he had first discovered the joys that could be found with a woman. She had been older than him, a great catch in his eyes, and she had taken her duties as his bedmate seriously.

She had helped him make certain that the next Lord of the Aminabad Desert was as formidable in bed as he was anywhere else, a man of myth and legend wherever he roamed. She had done her job well.

So too would these women, he knew.

He only wished he could give his the same attention.

By the time the sun set, leaving trails of bright lights in the sky behind it as it went, Cyrus had given up pretending to tend his responsibilities. Instead he waited in the King's traditional chambers, connected to the harem by one hall that had no other entry or exit. Back in antiquity, blind guards had lined this hall as the King sampled his wares, making certain that no one else dared look upon the royal bounty.

He felt the weight of all that history work within him like heat as he stood in the ancient rooms, staring at the same statues and mosaics that a long line of his ancestors must have gazed upon just as he did now. All of his windows along one wall were archways that led onto a balcony that looked down into the harem courtyard, where kings of old had stood in their time and selected which women they wished might join them of an evening. Some even made them fight for the honor. They had also watched their children run and play here, protected from any who might rise against them, for the fortress boasted the most impregnable walls in the whole of the kingdom.

No one had ever breached the fortress. No one ever would.

By the same token, of course, no one ever got out, either.

As his father had reminded him when he'd brought Cyrus here.

In many ways, Cyrus knew that he was a modern man. He had his Western education. He had his Western blood, for that matter. He liked books from all corners of the globe and was not opposed to Western entertainment—for if his time at university had taught him anything, it was that one should not critique things blindly. For that could only and ever lead to knee-jerk reactions and such responses were beneath him. Far better to understand why people enjoyed such things, so that any critique would necessarily be of what any given thing *actually was*. Not what he feared it might be.

And so, though he had learned right here that women

like the mother he had adored could hide betrayal behind their smiles, he had not rushed to judge Hope after her father died and she hadn't come to him. He had watched. He had waited.

He had learned today that she truly intended to walk to that altar and marry another. Only when she had gone to such lengths to show him who she was had he acted upon that information. And yet even then, had honored the promises that had been made to her father and married her, though it could have been argued she deserved no such consideration.

In truth, what happened between them now was justice.

The sort women who hid behind their softness, their prettiness, could not deserve.

But Cyrus did not seek justice because it was or was not deserved, he told himself then, but because it was no more and no less than *just* and therefore *right*.

And he could think of no reason at all that he should see Hope wave that languid hand of hers in his head then, as if laughing at him once again. When no one else had dared, not since he was small.

He heard the sound of the harem doors opening then, but he did not turn, because there were old songs in his head once more. He waited them out, taking notes of the sounds he actually heard here and now, keenly aware that it must have sounded just like this centuries before. Her bare feet against the cool tile. The swish of her silks against her skin.

The scent of her reached him first, that hint of spice

and a warm, heady fragrance that made him think of flowers that bloomed only in the dark.

"Sire, all is as you wish it," his man told him with the usual deference.

Cyrus turned then and felt himself go still.

For Hope Cartwright had been dangerous enough when she had existed only in photographs. She had been astonishingly perilous when he'd put his hands upon her, tossing her over his shoulder and carrying her away from the scene of her perfidy. Dressed in a wedding gown meant to be removed by another man, she had been something like a siren—even to him, who should have been immune.

But all of that faded to insignificance next to *this*.

Hope Cartwright, dressed in the King's silks with jewels gleaming in her navel and at her throat. She wore a pair of loose, billowing trousers that he knew only suggested the shape of pants and were mostly there to protect a woman's most secret places from any stray glances of anyone who was not him. Her golden hair tumbled down all around her, brighter and more lustrous that he could possibly have imagined. Her breasts were caught in a kind of bodice that held them aloft, the same rich color as the pants, and everything else was bare.

Bared to his gaze. Bared *for* his gaze.

These truths were like a roaring within him.

He was filled with the sudden, primitive fury that his man had gazed upon her like this. He understood at last the distasteful old practice of blinding the harem guards. But he shuttered these strange furies even as they beset him. He nodded at the loyal retainer who had served him so well and stayed where he was, still and in control of himself, as the other man quit the room.

At last.

"I didn't realize when you said *harem* that you intended to go full tilt at it." Her voice was bright. As if this was that holiday she'd mentioned. She even flashed that outrageous, heedless smile at him. "Complete with outfits."

Because, of course, she would treat even this as something deserving of that jocularity she prized so much. Clearly she did not understand the significance of where she was. Much less what she wore.

He studied her, ordering his flesh to obey him. Ordering his sex to behave. He folded his arms, not at all certain he liked the creature this woman made him.

As if she was the one in control here, not him.

But his father had taught him the futility of wishes and the scourge of weakness, beating his own out of him in the years he stayed here, and he had not survived all of that to bend now. He no longer regarded those years as a cruelty. They had been a kindness. They had taught him, and well. He would not repeat the mistakes of the past. He would not allow a woman to get between him and his kingdom.

His children would not cry their unworthy mothers, burying their faces in their pillows in the dark of night.

He had married this woman, but he would not let her ruin him.

Cyrus watched as she took her time looking away from him, and catalogued—distantly, he told himself—the flush that appeared on her cheeks, telling him that despite the effect she had on him, she was truly only a woman, in the end.

As susceptible as any other woman was to him, and always had been.

He would do well to remember that.

She was staring at the great bed that stood at the far end of the room, in its own kind of alcove so massive that the posters that surrounded it seemed to go nearly up to the ceiling itself.

"Will we get right to it, then, after all?" she asked the same bright voice. "Is this more of an immediate total immersion situation or is it better to ease our way in and see what the water's like…?"

He raised a brow, finding himself perhaps too pleased when she flushed again. "If that is your wish. I assumed that perhaps we might share a meal, *omri*. But by all means, if you would prefer to begin offering me the gifts we discussed before…?"

She laughed, but this time the sound seemed tinged with the faintest hint of hysteria. Something he found he also liked, because unlike the dryness and the arch amusement, a touch of hysteria in these circumstances seemed appropriate. For her.

"As a matter fact, I find I'm starving." Her gaze found his, again. "I am slightly concerned that this is part of your plan. Making me hungry to the death."

Cyrus could have told her that was, indeed, part of his plan. But he did not mean to ignite the hunger she was talking about.

"I am delighted to offer you a stay of execution," he told her instead, though he wasn't sure why he was bothering. Not when, clearly, the notion of rolling about on his bed was all she could think about. But then, he could use that to his advantage.

He could use all of this to advantage. And wasn't that the point?

Cyrus led her out from the bedchamber into the rest of his apartments, leading her up the small stone stairway that climbed a wall on the far exterior side, then wound its way out onto the fortress's roof.

On either side of the fortress, the battlements stood and were manned by his guards. But this was the King's personal watchtower. Too many of his ancestors had stood here before him, gazing out at the mighty desert that provided the Aminabad people with their wealth and staved off their challengers in turn. His own father had viewed this tower as a retreat. The one place he could come and get himself right with the desert that made them all.

Tonight Cyrus had ordered his people to prepare the very top of the tower, surrounded by its thick walls that allowed a man to keep safe while he viewed the onslaught of attacking armies, for an intimate dinner.

He saw at once that they had outdone themselves. It was an Arabian Nights fantasy come true, as ordered. There were rugs on the floor, colorful pillows tossed this way and that, and too many candles to count. In the center, on low, round tables, a feast to feed an army had been laid out on gleaming platters.

And despite what she'd said below in the bedchamber, Cyrus had watched this woman stuff herself on the plane. He had spent his formative years with a woman who had professed herself full to the gills if she ate an entire salad, and he half expected Hope to do the same sort of thing now. To take one look at the platters piled high with roasted meats, cheese and honey, dishes containing savory and sweet pastries alike, and confess that she was not quite so hungry after all.

But that was not Hope.

Because unlike his mother, who had viewed all food with suspicion and particularly tempting food with outright horror, Hope made a small sound that sounded a great deal like a squeal at the sight of the feast awaiting them. Then she flung herself down on one of the cushions and did not wait for him to join her as she dug in.

This was a good thing, because he found he needed a moment to compose himself. For there was something wildly erotic about watching a woman indulge her appetite so thoroughly. So recklessly. And with such merry abandonment.

What would it be like, he found himself wondering, to take a woman with an appetite such as this to his bed? Was this the reason why she had found herself incapable of keeping her promises to him? Was she so voracious, so carefree and enthusiastic in all things, that she could not be contained by a vow to a single man?

Even though the very idea was anathema to Cyrus in practice, there was something about the notion that got to him anyway. A woman whose art was sensuality itself, in whatever form it took. A woman who deserved appreciation, for such an art was a gift in truth.

A woman who it would be some kind of sin to lock

away forever, starving her of all the materials she needed to create her masterpieces—

But he shook that off. Cyrus was not a man who could allow himself to indulge even the faintest hint of weakness. Not even if it first came to him in the guise of something else entirely—and maybe especially not then.

He ordered himself to eat sparingly, and with no particular *sensuality.*

And it was only when she was finished, when she sat back and made a lusty sort of sound that set everything in him alight, that he decided it was time to remind them both why they were here.

That her appetites were to be used against her, not indulged.

Not even by him.

"I regret to inform you," he told her coldly, the better to keep the bulk of his fury hidden because a leader did not lower himself to *displays*, "that the man you wished to marry today did not tear apart the Italian countryside in pursuit of you when you were taken. He did not even follow you out of the chapel. I am to understand that what he did instead was gaze about the assembled witnesses until he could choose a different woman to wed in your stead. They were married within the hour."

Across the low table, gleaming in the golden candlelight, Hope paused in the act of licking honey from her fingers. Yet Cyrus could not read the expression in her gaze. He only noted some emotion or other before she looked back down again.

He did not like that much at all.

"Have you nothing to say?" he growled at her. "Or is it that you do not wish to show me, the man you have betrayed so terribly, what it feels like to be betrayed again in turn?"

He saw her shoulders shake slightly and felt a stab of something that very nearly felt like guilt—but could not be, for what had he to feel the least bit guilty about? He was not the one who had broken promises. That she was here at all indicated that he alone had kept them.

Still, something in him turned over too quickly, because he hadn't imagined she *could* weep, this shockingly unbothered girl who did not seem to apprehend her own peril—

And when she raised her face toward his again, he could see that her eyes were bright, indeed.

But not with tears.

With laughter.

She was *laughing.*

"The thing is, you actually did me a great favor, Cyrus," she told him. And laughed more at his expression. Then harder when he began to scowl. "I'm sorry if you thought I might throw a fit of some kind. I won't. All I *can* do is thank you."

CHAPTER FIVE

EVEN IF SHE hadn't meant what she said, Hope probably would have found a way to say it anyway if she'd known that doing so would leave that stunned expression on Cyrus's absurdly handsome face.

She was only human, after all. And she hadn't had anything much in the way of fun since before her father died. This was the closest she was likely to get.

The upside was, it really did feel like fun just now—though she supposed that could be all the sweets she'd inhaled.

"I beg your pardon?" Cyrus asked, his voice still in that growly register that seemed to burrow deep into her veins, crawling all over her from the inside out.

Speaking of things that were also fun, in one way or another.

"Lionel and I had an arrangement," she told him when his scowl began to tip over into fully thunderous. "It was business, not pleasure."

Hope could admit that she was enjoying herself, even if what she should have been doing was worrying about her poor mother, on her own for the first time. Maybe it was just that her belly was full again. That she'd lost herself in tasting the sweetest honey she'd ever encountered, and it was impossible not to feel delighted by even the memory of that. Not to mention the sheer number of happy little candles flickering in the desert night atop this little tower, as if doing their best to hold on to that faint hint of remaining sunlight out there on the distant horizon like a few inside out smudges, quiet suggestions of the day that would not dawn for hours.

Or maybe it was as simple as the dark, consuming way that this man who claimed she was his wife looked at her, as if he intended to eat her whole. Possibly tonight.

That was enough to make anyone giddy.

"He had no interest in sharing a life with me." Hope waved a hand in Cyrus's general direction, which felt unwise. Perhaps that was why she did it. Twice. "Or even a bed. He comes from a very old family in Spain, you see, and his grandmother has a lot of opinions about what he should do and how he should present her with grandchildren at the first opportunity. He does not wish to do this. And as she is quite old, he intended to present me as his bride instead and tell her we planned to try to come up with a few grandchildren. In five years, if his grandmother was still with us, we agreed that we would address ourselves to the issue of creating an heir, likely still not in a bed. But it was his fervent hope—and mine—that none of that would ever come to pass."

"You cannot possibly expect me to believe this…fiction." Cyrus's voice was the barest scrape of sound and yet still it seemed to scrape like a knife's sharp edge against her nerves.

And other parts of her.

"Why would it be fiction?" She was still replete from all the food she'd eaten and the honey still in her tongue. She was still tempting fate by lying there dressed in very little silk, waving her hand *languidly* as if she imagined she might be safe. "Why would I bother to tell stories in the first place?"

"Why does anyone lie?" He made one of those faces that he was so good at, she knew already. It managed to suggest that he *could have* delivered a dissertation on *her* lies, but was holding himself back by sheer force of will. "I cannot answer this for you, because I have always prided myself on telling the truth, no matter how unpalatable."

And she was already living dangerously. There seemed to be no particular reason to stop now.

"Have you ever noticed that the people who say things like that *mostly* just want an excuse to be rude?" She smiled when he flashed that particular affronted look at her, as if no one dared say such things to him. Why did she think that meant she ought to be the one who did? When it wasn't clear that she wouldn't spend the rest of her life in some kind of prison? "I'll take that to mean you hadn't noticed. But I'm betting you will now."

"I'm glad that you find this as amusing as you do everything else." Cyrus neither looked nor sounded the slightest bit *glad*. Much less amused. "I hope you may always find it so. But I doubt very much that it will be possible."

"Yes, because of harems and not being allowed to have your sons, and all the rest of it." She almost laughed again, but checked herself when his dark eyes gleamed in a manner that felt a good deal like retribution. Hope made herself frown instead. "That all sounds terrible. But really, what I'm most worried about is my mother."

That part was not only not really a laughing matter, it was true. The fact that she had no idea what messes Mignon was making *even now* could, if she let it, become like a kind of rash that would sweep over her and make her start…prickling.

She did not need to start *prickling* in front of this man.

What she needed was Mignon safe.

And Hope knew that Cyrus knew all about her mother by the way he sighed. He reached over to pick up his drink, then took a moment to swirl the liquid around in its glass. Juice, not alcohol—and that made perfect sense to her.

Cyrus Ashkan did not strike her as a man who wished to soften his senses. For any reason. Because he was clearly a man who gloried in his control over himself and everything around him.

Not because he feared that others might use his dulled senses to take advantage—which was why Hope never touched alcohol. She couldn't imagine what might have become of her over the past few years if she'd indulged.

Cyrus did not look at her when he spoke. "I cannot think why you would trouble yourself with fruitless worries about your mother. I'm not certain that she has ever thought of anyone but herself in the whole of her life."

And Hope was still living her way through a very long, very strange day. It was hard to fathom that just this morning, she'd been close to tearing out her hair over her mother in a villa in Lake Como, as ever.

But she had spent hours upon hours since in the most outrageously decadent spa of all time. If this was what harems were like, she kept thinking as she was handed from one marvelous treatment to the next, then it was clear that she'd been sold a pack of lies her entire life. Because this harem was delightful.

She'd been massaged until her muscles felt like butter. She been fussed over at every turn. The little sting of this or that treatment had been quickly soothed away. She been bathed and then oiled, her hair brushed and styled, and when all that was finished they'd topped off the experience by wrapping her in the finest silk she'd ever felt against her skin.

Hope had never felt so nurtured in her life.

And maybe that was why she found herself thinking about her mother with all her usual sympathy, but now mixed in with an instant desire to defend her. Because *she* might think any number of things about her mother's failings. *She* might spend all the time she liked totting up Mignon's shortcomings, because she did all of that with love.

Hope really didn't want to hear these things from anyone else.

Especially not a kidnapper.

"My mother was raised to be a trinket," she told him, feeling less languid. More serious. Maybe even something like vulnerable, though she was sure that wasn't wise. "My grandparents were very old-school, by all accounts, and they taught her that her job, her single purpose on this earth, was to be pretty. To make everyone around her gaze upon her like she was a lovely piece of art and expect nothing of her except that she should sit on her shelf and be looked upon. So that was what she did."

She felt as if her voice filled the night around them, calling down the tangle of stars above. Making the desert night feel like an embrace shot through with just enough starlight, like inverted candles, so everything was a part of that same fire.

And Cyrus was looking at her intently—maybe too intently—so she continued. "My father adored her. He loved her at first sight and every time he looked at her thereafter, he loved her more. Or so he told everyone he encountered." She swallowed then, because this part was harder. More complicated. "And when he died, she didn't know what to do. On an epic scale. She has spent the years since trying to find someone else who understands her particular provenance. And who will want to treat her as my father did. But the trouble is, she can't tell the difference between a man who only wants to look at a pretty thing for an evening or two and the kind of man who will make her the centerpiece of his world. His first, best collection, if you will. So it's been one heartbreak after the next."

"Heartbreak is one word for it, yes," he said, his voice colder than should have been possible for any number of reasons, starting with the fact that they were in the desert. "I know a little something about women who are considered nothing more than adornments. I cannot say that there is much to them behind the scenes. My own mother was hardly an exemplary human, so determined was she to keep me away from my birthright. She would have done better to pay more attention to the sort of trinket she was meant to be, I think."

Hope did not follow that up the way she wanted to, by pointing out that he had an entire other birthright he chose to ignore, back there in England with that mother he seemed to loathe so much. Somehow she understood that he would not be open to the subject.

"You can call it whatever you want. Heartbreak or otherwise, it doesn't change anything. She is who she is. But she still isn't any good on her own, you see, and she needs me to take care of her. That's the only promise I made my father before he died. It was part of my agreement with Lionel." She looked for some softening on Cyrus's face of sheer, impassive bronze, but there was nothing. She might as well have turned her face the other way entirely, so she could stare out into the desert. It was about as soft and inviting. "I was prepared to act the part of his wife to cater to his grandmother's wishes if he made sure that my mother was taken care of for the rest of her life. It was an easy exchange."

And it seemed easier now, so far away from having to enact it. So far away from that little chapel and the man who had glowered with annoyance as she'd drawn near. And who had still been the best of all the options available to her.

She'd considered that wedding, that man, her *triumph.*

And Hope wasn't sure that she would call this any sort of victory, this odd so-called wedding she'd had on a sandy tarmac today. But at least the way Cyrus looked at her did not suggest that he was *annoyed.* "That is not what I will require from you, *omri,*" he said.

Again, there was that sardonic inflection when he said that word. *Omri.* She had said it herself in the baths earlier and one of the women had sighed as if it was romantic, then whispered, *my life.*

Hope had not had the heart to tell her that she thought the King meant it a bit more like a life sentence.

"I cannot abide acting," he was saying. "Or falsehoods of any kind."

"And according to you, you've already announced that I am your wife and that makes it as legal as any contract I could sign."

He looked as close to amused as she'd seen him so far. "More legal than any such document, for I am certainly considered a far more trustworthy source than your average barrister."

But marrying a man had always been her leverage. The worry for Mignon that had been kicking around inside her—if tamped down by an unexpected spa afternoon—seemed to intensify, then. It bloomed throughout her like a new rash altogether.

"Tell me what I need to do to make sure that my mother has what she needs," she said, and tried to force a smile. Not well, if his expression was any guide. "You've already gone ahead and kidnapped me. You've already carried me off to your lair, conveniently located in the middle of a desert. Tell me what it is I can give you. What it is that you *want* from me."

And for what seemed like a small eternity, there was only the starlight. The matching intensity in his midnight gaze.

The *gifts* he'd mentioned earlier seeming to simmer there between them.

"You must realize that I can take anything and everything I want, if I so wish," he said, very quietly.

But she didn't tense up at that, or get scared. Mostly because she *wasn't* scared, she realized in the next moment, the way she would have been upon hearing similar statements from other men—and it was because he wasn't other men.

He was Cyrus Ashkan and he was not threatening her. He was making a statement of fact.

A simple statement of undeniable fact that was, in its starkness and his quiet restraint, a demonstration of the power she'd felt emanate from him even down the length of that long chapel aisle.

A power he could have used against her already, but hadn't. Oddly enough, that made her feel as close to safe as she had since her father died.

It hummed in her like a new heat all its own.

Cyrus inclined his head slightly, as if he could read in her precisely what he wished to see there. She didn't know why she hoped he could. "Yet all I want from you is a kiss, Hope. Just one kiss."

"A kiss?" She couldn't breathe, suddenly. She told herself it was the dry air. "But…why?"

It was as if he knew she would ask that. His harsh face altered as his stern mouth…curved. Just slightly. "To see the truth of who we are, you and me. That's why."

Hope was not at all certain she wanted to know who she was, just then. Not when it felt like this—like a sudden rush of heat inside of her, so overwhelming that she wasn't sure if she would actually manage to remain sitting up straight. Or as close to straight as she was managing, propped up on all these pillows.

She had been so busy gorging herself, again, that she'd been able to tell herself she'd missed the sensuality that seemed to hang in the air between them. That desire she hadn't known was in her until today that she'd managed, somehow, to tuck back in its place again while she was buffed to a shine. And though she knew that there were guards and staff spread out all over this fortress, up here on the top of this tower it was only them. The nearest other people were the lone guards who walked the segments of the battlements down below.

Otherwise it was only the two of them, alone in the silken night. The two of them, cast in the light of so many flickering candles. The two of them splayed out on the floor beneath a ceiling of careless stars, no matter how many bright pillows were festooned about here and there.

No matter if Hope could breathe or not.

"I make it a personal policy not to kiss men who dislike me," she told him, trying to summon some kind of authority as she spoke. But she didn't think she got there. Not in the face of all the power he managed to generate simply by…staying where he was, seemingly at his ease as he lounged there opposite her.

Though that hard gleam in his dark eyes and that sense of hovering danger all around him suggested otherwise.

"Do you indeed?" he asked her, without the slightest indication that he was even attempting to conceal the fact he was challenging her.

This is who you are, he had said to her in a different country today, as if she had betrayed him when she still hadn't known his name. And he hadn't stopped there. *You do not even care what man claims you, do you? You flit from one to the next as if it is nothing.*

And she couldn't understand why she didn't feel more offended. Why she hadn't then. Why she didn't now. Surely it said something about her that his accusations didn't seem to land like the blow she knew they should be.

Then again, maybe she was more like her mother that she'd ever imagined possible.

Hope couldn't say she particularly liked *that* line of thought. Had she really gone through all of this—all the struggle of the past years—to be no more than a man's bauble, in the end? Perhaps loved in her time, but in the end, as disposable as any other bit of tat a man collected over the course of his life and left behind when he was gone?

To be tossed out or packed away as it suited whoever came next?

Imagining such a future made her feel cold.

Hope made herself sit up straighter, as if that could somehow draw attention away from the pillows strewn about. Suggesting that in this place, the lines between things were blurred in advance. No need to worry about how a person got from point A to point B when all the points were mashed together like this. If there was no differentiation between eating dinner and rolling on the floor, it was all part and parcel of the same sensuous experience—

But she didn't like the way her body was responding to that line of thought. She didn't care for the way a sweet sort of shiver, like its own sort of honey, snaked along her arms. Or the way her nipples seemed to join in, hardening against the silk that barely covered them and making that, too, feel like a caress.

She *really* didn't like the fact that all of that melting heat that she could feel inside her wound its way down the length of her, spiraling around and around until it became a bright, hot problem between her legs.

And Hope knew a whole lot about men. More than anyone should know, to her mind. All of her interactions with men had been inside out—she understood that now. There was her father, who she had loved beyond reason, and on the other side there were… all the other men. All the ones Mignon had brought home, who had leered at Hope when she should have been too young for them to notice her. All the men she had taken it upon herself to interview over the past few years, who had shown not the slightest shame in sharing with her every last bit of the depravity that animated them. They had all been so *proud*, in fact.

All of them.

She understood now, when it already felt too late, that she was missing a crucial bit of her education.

Because never before had a man looked at her and made her feel like *this*.

Her father had looked at her with fondness and adoration, and she had bloomed in his regard. Then missed him when he was gone. Other men looked at her and she cringed. She had flushed with disgust on more occasions than she could count. Her heartbeat had always kicked into high gear, usually because she was worried for her safety in one way or another.

She had thought of Lionel Asensio as a savior because he had looked at her as if he was examining produce at a market. That had felt much colder and therefore safer than anything she'd experienced before him.

Cold was not how she would describe the way this man looked at her.

"I think you're trying to intimidate me," she said quietly.

"*Omri*, please. Do not mistake the matter. I do not need to try." That should have been even more intimidating, and yet somehow, it was the opposite. Because she knew by now that the bullies didn't sit around playing games or *talking* about these things. They bullied. That was exactly what they did, always. "We are here, in a fortress so impregnable that its very name makes my enemies weep. For they know that whatever it is that waits here, they can do nothing. And have you not been treated well, Hope?" Was it her imagination that he seemed suddenly…closer than before? "Why is it that you imagine I would go to the trouble of tending to you if I planned now to tear you apart?"

She did not think he intended to do that. Exactly. But she was caught up in the way the light danced over his bronze features and she could not begin to explain why it was that *looking* at him made her ache. In ways she couldn't make sense of, even to herself.

"Is that not what men do?" she asked softly. "I thought the purpose of all of this was to punish me. To make me pay for breaking a promise I can't even remember."

"Can't you?"

She laughed at that, though she felt significantly less amusement than before. "You have no idea what I've been through these past years. If I'd had the slightest idea that there was some Prince Charming hanging around, waiting to rescue me—"

But she stopped, suddenly.

Maybe it was the *Prince Charming* bit, reminding her of all the daydreams she'd been thrusting aside on her way down the aisle today in Italy. Maybe it was because her full stomach and the soft light had lulled her into sense of security, the first she'd felt in a long, long while.

Hope couldn't tell what it was, but all of a sudden, memories of her father swept through her. When she'd been a little girl and would find him in the evenings after her bath in that cozy study of his, lined with books, smelling of cigars he loved, and, in her memories at least, always sporting a happy fire in the grate. He had always welcomed her with that jolly laugh of his, opening up his arms so she could run into them.

Then she snuggled against him, sitting there in that cozy armchair before the fire.

When she was older and thought of herself as far too old for sitting in laps she would tuck herself into the chair across from his, so he could look at her with his kind, wise eyes as he listened to her prattle on about her prosaic days as if worlds hung in the balance.

Sometimes, even now, she would think of that study and his obvious, open love for her as she drifted off to sleep. Sometimes she thought she could almost catch his scent, or feel his arms around her, or hear his laughter in her ears again.

But tonight she found herself remembering the stories he would tell her when she complained that her life was boring or sad, for reasons she couldn't fathom now. The stories were bright and happy, about the life she would lead, joyful and sweet.

They were usually some or other take on how she might not have been a princess herself in the eyes of the world, but was her papa's princess, all the same.

And a princess like my Hope deserves to have a fine prince of her own. She could hear her father's voice so clearly now, so distinctly. *Wouldn't that be nice?*

After he died, she had remembered those stories, but had thought nothing of them. They were just stories, after all. Just fairy tales a lovely man had told his daughter. There was no harm in them—and no truth, either.

For she had learned quickly enough that there was no point believing in fairy tales. Not the kind that people told these days, anyway. Real fairy tales were different, of course. They were dark and grim, and there was nothing cozy or safe about them at all.

Hope had learned that the hard way.

It had never occurred to her, until this moment, that there could possibly be a kernel of truth in those stories her father had told her.

That there could possibly be a prince after all.

She pushed back from the low table, then onto her feet, before she realized that she meant to move. Hope looked wildly around as if she might find an explanation for this in the candlelight, on the table itself, or even on the uncompromising face of the man who only watched her, his gaze hooded.

But with an unmistakable satisfaction stamped all over him.

"Perhaps your memory is not so faulty after all?" he asked softly.

Dangerously.

As if he could read her so easily when he remained a mystery to her.

And as she watched—not sure if she was taken aback or something far more complicated—he unfolded himself from that lounging position and rose to his feet with a breathtaking grace, fluid and athletic at once.

"My father used to tell me stories," she said, maybe too quickly, though without any real idea why she should find herself confessing anything. "But I never thought..."

"There are contracts, Hope."

"There were no contracts in his office." She shook her head, thinking of all the papers she'd gone through, the folders upon folders she'd thrown away. Could she have missed something? After all, it was unlikely to have been marked *Prince Charming Is Not a Fairy Tale*. Had her escape been in her reach from the start? Hope could barely cope with that idea. "Who could possibly think that princes in foreign lands and kingdoms I'd never heard of were anything but stories?"

He studied her for what felt, to her, like a lifetime.

"Perhaps what you say is true. That you did not know you were mine. For I am many things." His voice was like the night. Like the desert all around. It was within her as well as without. It was taking her apart without him having to so much as lift a finger. "And many stories have been told about me. But the only tale you need tell yourself is this: that whatever you knew or did not know, you are here now. Where you belong. And you are my wife, as was promised long ago. A prince now a king in a place that is very real, who wants only a kiss. Is that story enough for you?"

And she could see that he meant that as another challenge. Maybe even a warning a wise woman would heed. But Hope felt the strangest sensation wash over her, then. So strange that she knew it was mad even as she thought it.

But…if all those fairy tales her father had told her were true, then why not all fairy tales?

Maybe she really should kiss him, here and now, because wasn't that how spells were broken? Maybe if she kissed him, everything would go back to the way it was.

Maybe if she kissed him, with all these feelings she'd shoved down deep inside her, she could turn back time.

So she would never have to find her father unresponsive in that study that had always been about their coziest family moments. Her mother dancing to the music her father played for her. Her parents sometimes dancing with Hope held between them, as if that kind of joy could last forever if they all sang along.

Maybe all of this was a dream. A terrible dream, nothing more.

Maybe if she kissed an impossible man on top of a magical tower, surrounded by candles and beneath the stars, she could wake up at last.

So Hope didn't think.

She closed the distance between them, and she didn't stop at that. She threw herself at Cyrus, knowing on some instinctive level that he would catch her—

And he did.

Hope was aware of the strength in his arms, and how that chest of his felt even more like a stone wall now than it had earlier today, when he had carried her so easily away from the cold life she'd seen as a reprieve.

Bracing herself against the hard ridges of his abdomen, she tipped back her head as she surged up onto her toes.

And she thought, *If this is a fairy tale, the spell should be broken.*

So Hope leaned up as best she could and kissed the Prince who had become a king, just like her father had told her she would long ago.

CHAPTER SIX

HOPE KNEW TWO things immediately.

One, that this was not the spell she had imagined it was, because his mouth was both harder and softer than she ever could have conceived when she pressed her lips to his.

And two, that this was magic all the same.

It was true that the world didn't explode into a shower of stars that turned into small dancing creatures. There was no magic wand or sudden swell of music.

But there was heat. Almost too much heat to bear.

When she made as if to step back, his arm went around her and hauled her even closer against him. And then she stopped worrying about what was happening, or what was magic and what wasn't, because his mouth opened against hers and it was so *good* and everything seemed to slide into that same spiral of sensation that was winding tighter and tighter within her.

Cyrus licked his way along the seam of her lips, silently commanding her to open for him. And she shivered, but she did. And though she felt hesitant, maybe, and yet wild at the same time—everything seemed to feel *right* when his tongue stroked hers.

She hadn't understood, before, how a kiss could involve *a whole body*.

Hope was *aware* of him in a thousand different ways.

There was the spicy scent of him, all around her, like the candlelight flickering over them both. And more, the profound and alien *maleness* of him—of his body, of the way he held her, of the differences between his mouth and hers.

That he felt so hard when she felt soft, and softer by the second.

She was aware of herself, too, in whole new ways. There was a driving need between her legs, but that was only part of it. Her breasts felt rounder and softer even as her nipples hardened against his chest. And her body seemed to make up its own mind about what it should do, because she found herself pressing against him, rubbing herself into him, so caught up in the way all these different sensations made her feel—the mad storm of it all—that she found herself making greedy little noises in the back of her throat.

And all the while, his mouth moved over hers, with hers.

Hope didn't have to have had sex herself to understand that the way he thrust his tongue into her mouth, over and over again, mimicked that action.

So well and with such delirious heat that she could feel a kind of throbbing in the core of her, as if her body was readying itself for that most intimate invasion.

And perhaps the true magic was, after failing to understand why her mother let all those men get close enough to break her heart, Hope finally got it.

She finally understood completely.

Because she thought in these wildly hot moments, with all the careening sensations setting her alight, that she had never wanted anything more than to tear off her clothes and his and do whatever was necessary to wrap herself all over him, take him inside her, and follow the sweet hunger wherever it led.

And it took her too long to understand that he was laughing, a dark and rude and yet stirring sound, when he set her away from him.

"I don't..." she began, shaking her head, though that failed to clear it. There was too much sensation still kicking around inside her, and for some reason she wanted to cry, and yet all the while there was an ache that only seem to grow and grow—

But then there was the way he was looking at her. That made her want to curl up into a ball. And cry for different reasons altogether.

"Cyrus?" she whispered.

He moved past her, still laughing in that way that made the back of her neck prickle.

"I will give you this, *omri*," he said, his voice much too dark and that word like a gut punch. "I can certainly see why you are so popular."

And then, without a backward glance, he left her there.

There on top of that tower, alone in the desert night—and it took Hope far too long to understand what had happened.

First she stayed where she was, her breath coming so fast and so hard that it made the silks she wore move against her, which didn't help her oversensitized skin.

She thought he would return, but instead the women came, murmuring things in low voices she found she was happy she didn't understand. They led her back down into the fortress, down the stone stairs that wound away from the seductive night, the watching stars.

They took the same route through Cyrus's bedchamber, though he was nowhere to be found. And they did not stop at his towering bed, leading her instead into the harem, lit up with soft lanterns and the sound of tumbling water.

It was there, tucked up in the little alcove of a room they'd told her was hers in her soft and welcoming bed, that she pulled the airy blankets over her and let herself understand at last what that look Cyrus had given her meant.

Because it had been so scathing. Almost disgusted.

"He thinks that's how I am with every man," Hope whispered out loud, into the feathers of her pillow.

And there was still that part of her that wanted to curl up into the fetal position, rock herself the way she always did when her heart felt bruised, and soothe herself to sleep.

But she didn't.

Instead, Hope laughed.

And she kept on laughing for a long while, her whole body shaking with it and the faintest hint of moisture appearing in the corners of her eyes.

She laughed and she laughed, until the laughter

turned into all that heat and aching that coursed through her body and she couldn't seem to keep herself from running her hands over her own desperate skin. She found the hard pebbles her nipples had become and imagined her hands were Cyrus's, testing the weight of her against his palms and then slowly making their way over her ribs, her belly, until he reached that heat between her legs. She thought of the way his tongue had thrust between her lips, and even thinking about it made her shiver all over.

Hope followed that delicious shivering, dipping her own hands into the heat of her core and imagining that things had ended in a different way entirely up there in that tower. That Cyrus had taken her down into all those pillows, pushed her silks aside, and kept right on kissing her like that even as he thundered between her legs.

For surely he was a man who would always feel like thunder.

She was still laughing as the glory of it took her over, there alone in her harem bed, so she pressed her face into her own pillow and kept what magic there was to herself.

The next day, she woke to find the light streaming into the courtyard, making everything gleam like new. And she hadn't bothered to change out of the silks they'd given her when she'd fallen into bed, so she wore them as she padded out of her room to find herself alone with the great fountain as it babbled and burbled, making its own song into the morning. The courtyard was filled with trees that shouldn't grow in a place like this, ripe with fruit and covered in green, and there were even songbirds in their branches.

Hope supposed she should have felt scared, but she didn't. Instead, it was the first morning in a long, long while that she didn't feel the usual grinding panic of what she would do, how she would do it, *if* she *could* do what she must to keep herself and her mother safe.

Because there was nothing she could do here but… be here.

And there was a liberty in having no choices. Even if, deep down, she knew that eventually the panic would return to her—because Mignon was still out there, doing God only knew what in Hope's absence.

But if she thought about her mother, she would fall apart, and that wouldn't help her at all.

So she didn't.

She breathed in and out, again and again, and she didn't. She couldn't.

Mignon was a grown woman and Hope had to believe that she would find her way.

Because she couldn't allow herself to think anything else.

Her attendants found her there some while later, sitting beneath one of the trees while the fountain laughed, the birds sang, and the desert sun warmed her. They brought her rich coffee and decadent pastries, and so she had chocolate on her tongue and music in her ears when she looked up—caught by more of that magic, maybe—to find Cyrus standing in those arched windows in the King's bedchamber, looking down.

For what seemed like an eternity, Hope held his eyes with hers. She felt filled with his midnight gaze.

Captured as surely as she was in this harem.

He looked down at her, his face a study of ruthlessness, his gaze stern.

And that, too, felt like glory.

When he turned and walked away from his windows, Hope thought that despite everything, or maybe because of it, she was going to be far happier here than he might imagine. Because whatever else she might feel, she wasn't *afraid.*

And that felt more like freedom than it should.

As her days in the desert bled one into the next, that was exactly what happened.

Hope thought at first that Cyrus, having discovered what he clearly thought was proof of her promiscuity, would avoid her. But he did not.

Later that same day she was once again buffed to a gleam and brought before him. This time there was no tower beneath the stars, no pillows on the floor.

Instead, she joined him out on the battlements in the bright heat of the afternoon, and walked with him.

"I thought you had guards for this," she said as she walked beside him, grateful that she was not dressed only in those harem silks that bared most of her body. They had draped her in different garments, more enveloping, so that she might walk in the sun without burning to a crisp.

Though there was something electric about concealing so much of herself. It made Hope only too aware that she still wore that same silken harem outfit beneath it all.

Judging by the light in his gaze every time he looked down at her, she thought Cyrus felt that same electricity too.

"I ask nothing of the men who serve me that I'm not willing to do myself," Cyrus told her, sounding as forbidding as if she had suggested he lay about on couches, demanding peeled grapes, while his underlings fussed over him.

"I'm sure that that wins their loyalty," she murmured. Thinking that was an uncontroversial statement.

He stopped, and frowned down at her. "I do not attempt to *win* their loyalty." As if the very notion was outlandish. "They're loyal to me because I am the Lord of the desert. Because Aminabad rests between my hands and will do so for as many days as I draw breath. That is what wins their loyalty, *omri*. They would be loyal to me even if they hated me, because that is the way of my people. It is my role that matters."

"It was meant to be a compliment," Hope said mildly.

"You cannot understand." And his voice was clipped enough that it made her think that he was speaking to someone else. Not her. There was too much bleakness and outrage in his gaze for that. "My people do not put their loyalty up for grabs, or sell it to the highest bidder." He stood with his back to the great desert, scowling down at her. "I am the Lord of this desert not only because my father was, but because I earned it in sacrifice and struggle. I gave up more than you can imagine. All the softness within me, like songs. I tore them out and made myself what was required. These are the things that matter, Hope. Not *compliments*."

"I'll make a note to keep them to myself, then," she shot back, without thinking.

And then nearly jumped out of her skin when Cyrus moved toward her, backing her across the width of the battlements so that her own spine came into contact with stone. Still he kept coming, until he held her there.

Then he reached over to put his hand against her cheek. "I would work more with honey than vinegar, if I were you."

"You can't mean more kissing, surely." She made herself laugh as if he hadn't gone dark on her last night. As if he hadn't made more of his ridiculous accusations. "Though I don't know why you think I would bother to try when all it does is make you think the worst of me."

"I already think the worst of you. I married you anyway."

"Why? When you don't even believe me when I tell you the truth?" She was breathing too hard and she didn't like that he could see it.

"I believe that you didn't know," he said, as if the words cost him something—but not enough, Hope thought. Not quite enough. "What's done is done, *omri*. The choice you need to make is what kind of marriage this will be now we are in it."

She went as if to knock his hand away from her face, but something in the way his eyes glittered kept her from it. "I'm not sure what my impetus for that is, either. Didn't you tell me that the goal of all of this is to make me yearn endlessly for you while you parade about, impregnating other woman? Not exactly the lure you seem to think it is, Cyrus."

"And yet you yearn for me already," he said quietly. "Do you not?"

It was not a question. He knew.

She could see it all over him.

And it was not until she was back in the harem courtyard that Hope understood that it had been deliberate, on his part, to keep from kissing her then. He had gone out of his way to avoid it, in fact.

Because he *wanted* her to spend the rest of that afternoon and evening *lit up* with yearning for him.

He wanted her to lie in her bed just as she did that night, unable to sleep and thinking that there was nothing he did that didn't have a good reason—and that reason wasn't only making her *yearn.* The battlements themselves, for example. He had wanted her to see exactly how remote their location was. How there was nothing in any direction but sand and space, just as she'd feared when they'd first landed. She was well and truly trapped here, locked up tight until and unless he relented and let her go. Or didn't.

What he didn't understand was that Hope was resourceful. Maybe she couldn't extinguish that burning flame that flickered only for him, but she could play with it.

Especially if it helped her sleep.

"I don't think you really understand what's happening here," she told him a day or two later, sitting across from him at yet another low table. This one was in one of the numerous rooms that made up his expansive apartments. "England can rain on forever without me. I don't care if I ever go back. I certainly don't care that my wedding carried on with a different bride. It wasn't the groom or the ceremony I cared about. But I do need to know how my mother is faring. If I wasn't worried about her, I wouldn't mind in the least how long you plan to keep me here."

"You expend a great deal of energy on her," Cyrus observed, leaning back against another set of bright pillows, propping himself up on one elbow and looking like some kind of avenging angel.

Hope told herself that shouldn't make her feel like squirming where she sat. "She's my mother."

He only shrugged. "Everyone has a mother, Hope. Not everyone ties themselves into unnecessary tangles in service of their mothers. Quite the opposite, I would say."

"You say that as if it's perfectly normal to treat a mother the way you treat yours," she said, careful to keep her voice even. So he could not possibly take what she was saying as some kind of attack.

But she should have known better. When it came to the topic of his mother, he viewed everything as an attack. If she so much as mentioned his father, on the other hand, he was prepared to wax rhapsodic about the man's greatness ad nauseam. As if it was not possible to elevate one in his esteem without crushing the other.

Someday, she thought she might ask him why that was.

"I treat my mother as she deserves, no more and no less," he told her in that dark way that suggested she should not pursue the issue further. "And far better than some would do."

"It has always sounded to me as if she loves you beyond reason," Hope dared say, and then held her breath.

Because he looked at her as if she'd picked up the nearest statue and bashed him over the head with it. As if she'd said something horrid and vicious, and her heart thumped painfully in her chest as he stared back at her, letting her know that her emotions were far more engaged here than they should have been.

"That," Cyrus said when the silence between them grew so loud that Hope worried she might choke on it, "is not a word I would use when discussing my mother."

"You mean your father," Hope said, though she knew better, truly she did. "He was all harsh edges and ranting on about property rights, wasn't he? While your mother was wracked with anguish and only wondered how you were. It was in the documentary—"

And if he had been anyone else, she would have said that the look in his dark eyes then was something like fear.

But that was impossible. This was Cyrus Ashkan, Lord of the Aminabad Desert and all he surveyed besides.

"You are mistaking the matter," he told her, flatly. "My mother has always played well to a camera. And I think a great many people on this planet feel exactly about their mothers as I do about mine. I wouldn't be surprised if you did, too. The only difference is that I am not afraid to say so."

"I love my mother," Hope said quietly. "Neither one

of us is to blame for who we became because we lost my dad."

She thought that might shake something loose in Cyrus, remembering how shaken he'd looked for a swift moment there. Just that moment. As if he might open up about what had actually happened to him here. And for a beat, then another, of her heart, she thought he might.

Or better still, kiss her again in that stern and stirring way of his, all confidence and certainty and enough fire to set the world alight—

But he only lifted a hand and crooked her finger in her direction.

"I will let you call her, if you truly wish it," he told her, with great magnanimity. "But there is a price."

She told herself that she didn't know what she would do. She told herself that she took her time mulling it over.

But that was a lie.

She moved almost without thinking at all.

And it felt unseemly, the way she sighed in such a long-suffering fashion and then crawled her way around the low table. It felt significantly more dangerous than what had happened on the top of that tower.

Because they weren't standing. They were already lounging there, on the ground, and her breath caught as she imagined all the things that could happen in a position like this—

And how much she wanted those things to happen.

Hope could have pretended that she felt manipulated, but she didn't. All she'd wanted for days now was an excuse. All she'd wanted moments ago was for *him* to kiss *her.*

She thought he might sit up as she crawled to him, but he didn't. He merely waited for her. And gazed at her in pure challenge when she reached him, so that she moved closer still, angling herself very nearly *on top* of him—

But though she held herself there, shaking a little with the effort of suspending herself over him in such an awkward position, he didn't pull her closer. He didn't *do* anything.

"You must kiss me, Hope," he told her, sounded as if he was bored. She might have thought he truly was, were it not for that dark glittering thing in his gaze.

"Then it isn't a kiss freely given, is it?" she replied.

If she thought that might shame him, she was sorely mistaken.

"What makes you imagine you are free?" he asked. "What you are is mine."

And then all he did was wait, his midnight eyes gleaming bright, that curve of his mouth like a new heat inside of her.

She sat back and considered the problem. But there was nothing for it, because he had called her *his*, and it was a new storm that danced over her skin. Like a self-fulfilling prophecy. She tipped herself forward and slid her hands onto his chest, making no secret of the way she had to catch her breath as the sensation roared through her anew.

Hope leaned all the way over him again, but this time lowered herself so she was practically lying across his chest. The wall of his chest, all muscle and heat, that put the battlements to shame.

Then she leaned in even more and pressed her lips to his.

Just like before, there was that wild, spinning dizziness, all from the simple press of her mouth to his.

It felt like a song.

And then, after a moment or two of that alone, Cyrus took charge all over again.

He kissed her deeper this time, Wilder. He hauled her up against him and then turned, rolling her down into the pillows so that the weight of him was pressing into her.

And Hope…exulted.

His hands moved the way she'd imagined they might—never quite making it to her breasts or the greedy center of her need, but finding all the places that were exposed when the silks fell away.

Building fires wherever he touched.

All while he kissed her again and again—tutoring her, teaching her, tearing her apart.

She felt her hips rising up as if they were trying to find him. She snaked her arms around his neck, hauling herself even closer, trying to press every square inch of her body into his—

And it was no surprise, really, when he eventually set her aside again.

But this time, he was breathing just as hard as she was. And there was a certain fierceness in his gaze that would have made her shiver anew—

If she could tell the difference between one sort of shiver and another.

“Should I take it that this is you showing who you really are too?” Hope asked, because she couldn’t seem to stop herself.

And on some level she was aware that she clearly felt safe enough with this man that she thought she could be so reckless. That she could say such things without worrying about reprisals.

Cyrus bared his teeth into something she would never call a smile. It was too fierce. Too elemental. Then he rolled away from her and up onto his feet in a single swift move.

Once again displaying that particular grace that made him more dangerous and more sensual than any man should be all at once.

And as he stalked toward the door, she laughed dark and low, the way he had before. Hope pushed herself up onto her elbow, and watched him as he paused in the archway that led deeper into his chambers.

She decided to take it as evidence that he was as wrecked as she was that he had to reach out a hand to steady himself. Hope decided to view that as nothing short of a victory.

“Did you lie about giving me my one phone call from prison?” she asked, sounding far more bitter than she felt.

Because it was that or melt all over him, and even though she wanted to do nothing but, there was Mignon to think about.

Cyrus looked back at her, his eyes so dark they might as well have been black. Hope held her breath.

He said no other word, he simply walked from the room.

But before she could think to get back up onto her feet, to try to chase him down or argue the point, his man came and found her. He waited as she scrambled to her feet and then he led her into yet another room in these endless chambers. There was an armchair inside and a table with a phone on it.

The man dialed out, then handed her the receiver.

Hope took it numbly, staring at the old rotary phone as if she had never seen one before.

"One call is all you are permitted, by the grace of our lord and king," the man told her matter-of-factly. "I will be waiting just outside."

And Hope didn't know how she was supposed to process that Cyrus was the first man she'd met since her father had died who had actually kept his promises to her. Or the fact that there was still that same overwhelming storm stampeding about inside of her.

But the phone was ringing.

And there was a part of her, little though she might wish to admit it, that almost wanted to cry with the rush of joy and love and daughterly obligation when she heard her mother answer.

"It's me, *Maman,*" she made herself say instead. "Don't worry, *Maman*. It's me."

And she closed her eyes, wrapped her free arm around her middle, and braced herself as her mother began to wail.

CHAPTER SEVEN

SOME WEEKS LATER, Cyrus returned to the fortress from a necessary overnight trip down south to tend to the business of running his kingdom. He accepted the cold drink his staff pressed upon him upon his arrival, took his time showering as if he had felt no pressing need to rush back here, and then stood in the windows that overlooked the courtyard of his harem.

His harem with its single occupant.

He told himself that the project was an unqualified success.

Surely the fruit of this particular labor was ripe and sweet, no matter the uncomfortable questions she dared ask him on occasion. He had only to gaze down into the courtyard to assure himself of that.

The women danced below, all of them draped in flowing silks, but he knew precisely which one was Hope. He could see hints of that gleaming gold that drove him to distraction. Her hair. Her eyes.

All the other women danced well, as it was customary in Aminabad to learn these dances at their mothers' knees. It was a matter of hips and sweet elegance, finding the melody within them as they moved.

His wife—a word he still found sharp and strange, even in his own thoughts—was still learning. That was obvious even from a distance. And there was no denying that she did not possess the natural talents some of the others did.

Yet she was the one who mesmerized him.

Cyrus found himself transfixed. He could not look away.

But as soon as he realized how intently he stood there, how little it seemed possible he might ever drag his attention away, he forced himself to do exactly that. He tossed back the rest of his drink, the sweet cold juice he liked best, and hated that he found himself making pointless comparisons between the sugary hit of a mango and the taste of Hope's lovely mouth.

Of her kisses, greedy and demanding, that stole his sleep from him on too many nights to count.

The project might have been a success, by Cyrus's estimation, but Hope herself remained a puzzle. She was not afraid to negotiate with him, about anything and everything. Sometimes he thought she argued with him simply because she enjoyed it—when no one else would dare behave in such a manner. It was how he had agreed to allow her to call her mother each day, though he was not sure he liked it.

It was good that the older woman was doing better than Hope had imagined she would. Cyrus was pleased this was so, as it made Hope visibly happier and he found he was far more interested in her happiness than he should have been.

He had accepted that she hadn't known that she was promised to him. That her father had not told her directly and she had found no papers in his things—or, as she had confessed one night, perhaps she had but had not known what they were.

I was fourteen, she had said softly. *And I had to take on so many things.*

When Cyrus was fourteen, his father had decided it was a kindness to teach him how to survive sandstorms in the desert with nothing but a horse and a tarp. They had ridden toward the sand, not away, and Cyrus had spent long nights in between these sessions waking up in the night from dreams of sand filling his mouth, his nose, his eyes—

Or sometimes with tears on his face and his mother's songs in his head, something he had not admitted then and could not admit now, either.

That was the part of her keeping in touch with her mother that seemed to lead to more of those questions from Hope that he did not wish to answer.

Or maybe the deeper truth was that he did not know how to answer her, and he liked that even less.

You do not seem to have much use for mothers in general, she had said one night, walking with him in one of the gardens that were the pride and joy of the courtyards in this place. Gardeners from all over the kingdom competed for the chance to come here and make the fortress green in some small way as a way of celebrating and yet shifting the kingdom's past when this place really had been a military outpost.

Yet that night, the only bloom he had seemed able to focus on was Hope.

Don't be ridiculous, he had replied. *I hold mothers in general in the highest regard. Motherhood is a sacred state. Some claim it is the apotheosis of a woman's life.*

According to...women? Or according to the men who wish to lock them away to breed?

I do not wish to lock women *away.* He had frowned down at her. *You are the wife of the King, Hope. You could be taken and used against me by any enemies who might happen upon you. More than that, were I to allow such a thing to occur, it would paint me as a small, weak man, unworthy of the crown.*

As was typical with her, she had only smiled. *So it's only mothers, then. Only mothers who you can't abide.*

The only mothers I have paid the slightest bit of attention to in this life are yours and mine, he had told her shortly. *And it is not the fact they are mothers which offends me. It is that they are both dreadful at the only important jobs they have ever had.*

Hope had only looked at him in that way she did sometimes. As if he broke her heart.

My mother loves me unconditionally, she had told him. *What she might do or not do doesn't change that. You don't have to be a perfect person to love someone, Cyrus.*

And despite himself, he had been hit with another memory he went out of his way to lock down, far out of sight. He had been sixteen. It had been a long time since he'd woken in the night for any reason at all. But one night he and his father had journeyed to one of his father's minister's homes in the southern city, and Cyrus had been relegated to a guest room while the older men talked privately.

He'd seen the interview by accident. He'd been flipping through the channels, telling himself that he was merely cataloguing the sorts of things that rotted the minds of Aminabad subjects, and then there she was.

Until he saw her, he hadn't remembered it was his birthday.

I don't need it to be his birthday to remember him, she'd said, and though she hadn't been singing, her voice had gone through him all the same. Into him, like bone finding bone. *He's with me always. I hope he knows that.*

He'd felt as if someone had taken an axe to his head. He'd stood there, frozen in the guest room of a stranger's house, unable to move. He'd drunk her in on the screen before him. Her face, just as he recalled it. The anguish in her eyes.

The way she put her hands to her heart. *I love you, Justin,* she'd whispered, looking directly into the camera, her eyes filled with tears. *No matter where you are. No matter what. I will always love you.*

It had taken him so long to remember himself, to move from where he stood after the new program moved on, that his feet had fallen asleep beneath him. And it wasn't until weeks later that it occurred to him that she'd used the name he was meant to hate and reject.

What had shamed him since was that he'd never admitted what had happened to his father. And he'd played her words over and over in his head during the military exercises his father made him practice, to harden him, and the nights his father made him sleep alone on the bare floor of the fortress's dungeons, so he might understand that even that was a measure of his benevolence.

That his life was the gift his father had given him, and everything else was up to him to make his own.

He had told himself then, and since, that he was grateful for the lesson.

What he had never told a soul was that he had heard his own, lost name like a song all the while. As if it alone had sustained him. His mother's voice in his ear, his heart, his bones.

How he had always despised himself for the weakness.

Back then and that night with Hope in the garden, too. In the garden, he had stared at her until she looked away. Then he had told her that there would be a price if she wished to have closer contact with her own mother, and a greater one still if she insisted on mentioning his.

Cyrus could not pretend, now, he had not greatly enjoyed collecting on these prices she paid, but he had not expected that Hope would enjoy it so much too.

Oh, he had known that in the heat of things, she would want nothing more. That she would beg him to continue. He had never had any doubt on that score with any woman, not that he could seem to remember any others of late, and certainly not one who looked as if she was as fascinated with him as Hope always did.

But he had expected that when faced with the fact

that she wanted this man who she had been promised to and had therefore wronged, however unknowingly, she would shrink into herself and at least *pretend* she could not feel the heat between them.

Perhaps he would not even have blamed her.

Blame or not, he had expected her to feel shame.

Instead, she danced in the courtyard with the other women. Last he had heard, she had made friends of them all, and half the rest of the staff as well. Her laughter could always be heard in the halls and in the baths, until he began to wonder if he'd heard it on the wind down south, too.

Until he woke, craving the sound.

Cyrus had started to wonder why it was she never gave him what it was she'd given other men—and why it was he wanted her anyway. Had he been wrong about her dating life these past two years?

But no. He'd had the men she'd had all those dinners with extensively researched. He could not imagine any one of them would have let her slip between their fingers. Yet still he wanted her—and more by the day.

He had imagined that fulfilling his part of the promises made would be a coldhearted exercise, something he could compartmentalize as easily as he did everything else. With a swift and calculated seduction that would leave them both in precisely the places they belonged, as he'd explained to her at the start. He'd intended to give her the position her father had wished her to have, but nothing else.

None of it had gone as expected.

Because he'd met her, touched her, carried her from

that chapel. He'd tucked a scarf around her face to protect her from the desert sun. He had watched her laugh at him, more than once.

And there was nothing cold or calculated in the way they kissed.

He was quickly realizing that he wanted this wife of his far more than he should. Far more than was wise, as he had always been taught, for wanting was itself a weakness.

Something he was forced to reflect upon even more intently once he tore himself away from the dancing in the harem, settled himself in the office he used here, and tried to convince himself that he was neither besotted nor obsessed.

Which was hard to do when his man had asked him the very question he wished to answer least of all.

That of phase two of that original plan of his.

"I have assembled a slate of candidates, sire," his man told him, with obvious pride. "I have personally located the finest daughters of the finest men in the land. I have vetted the families myself, and I can tell you that not only are these women beautiful enough to be worthy of your notice, they are all eager for the opportunity to take their place in your harem and provide you with fine sons, so that the choice of the next Lord and King need not be made for them."

His own father had not been lucky in sons, something he and the whole of the country blamed on the woman who had stolen his firstborn from him. Whether that made sense or not had never mattered. Historically, the Lord of the desert tried to have as many sons as possible so he could, if necessary, make them into their own army. So had it been throughout the ages.

Cyrus did not feel he required an army. He tried to tell himself that was why he was not moving to fill his harem the way he'd planned to have done already.

"You have done fine work and I am pleased," he told his man.

The man placed a tablet before him. He indicated that all Cyrus needed to do was swipe this way or that to view pictures of the women on offer along with dossiers outlining precisely who they were and the benefits they would provide the kingdom if elevated to one of the Lord's wives.

Cyrus nodded along.

And later, after he had taken several phone calls and video conferenced with a number of advisors, he found himself flipping listlessly through the pictures. All the women ran together. They were beautiful, each and every one of them. But instead of congratulating himself that he had such loveliness to choose from, he found himself instead entirely too preoccupied with Hope.

As if he was the one imprisoned, songs in his head once more.

It was unsupportable.

It had to stop.

"It is time," he muttered to himself, staring out his window and seeing her face in place of the endless sand.

He had the staff prepare the usual dinner he would share with her, but this time, in his actual bedchamber. They arranged it in front of the grand fireplace, there to make tolerable and comfortable the winter nights that could made this old place of stone intolerably frigid.

As he had discovered by living without a fire on the nights his father wished to teach him that lesson, too.

Then Cyrus found himself waiting for her arrival like some kind of moonfaced swain. A notion that made him so tense, his jaw hurt.

This must end, he growled at himself.

And there was only one way he could think to make that happen. An exorcism of sorts, though he intended for it to be far more pleasurable.

He turned when he heard a faint sound behind him and nodded curtly at the guards who bowed to him from the antechamber.

But his eyes were on the woman who came in when they stepped aside.

Hope looked far less anxious than he thought she should. Not a hint of worry marred her brow. If anything, she looked happier every time he saw her.

Happy, healthy and sporting a sort of glow he found enraging, because he liked it.

She looked far more beautiful than she had when he'd taken her from that chapel. As if she was blooming here in his desert, and more by the day.

"You look even more ferocious than usual," she told him as she moved toward him, her hips a mesmerizing roll. One more thing she had learned down in the harem, he knew. And this thing, she was good at. Too good, perhaps. "A bit too grizzly for your own good, I'd say."

"It occurs to me that you're entirely too happy." He sounded dark and mean to his own ears. Worse, he sounded perilously close to out of control. "This is meant to be punishment, Hope. Not summer camp."

If he needed any further indication that things had gone astray, she didn't cower at that. She didn't seem to hear what he did in his voice. She didn't fling herself prostrate before him so that she might press her lips to the toe of his shoe, as he had seen his father's other wives do on many occasions. Not Hope.

Hope laughed.

And kept walking toward him, so that he almost thought she meant to do something—

But instead she passed him entirely, then flung herself down onto the pillows as if this was her chamber and he the interloper.

As if she had been the one to summon him here tonight.

As if the Lord of the desert could be *summoned.*

"The time has come to begin selecting other wives," he told her, realizing as he did that there was a part of him that wanted that information to...wound her, somehow.

In case he needed an unwelcome reminder that he was not as free in his ideas as he liked to think. Because if he had been raised here the way his father had intended and without the corrosive influence of his mother and his formative years abroad, surely such a notion would never have occurred to him.

Men in his position took as many wives as they pleased and women vied for the honor. When she expressed her hurt, he would view it as an outrage, because it was.

"Wonderful!" Hope cried instead. "Do I get to help you choose?"

And Cyrus found that this was the greater outrage by far.

Because she was not a woman of the Aminabad Desert. She should have reacted the way he'd expected her to react. With tears, at the very least. His memory of his mother's reaction to each new wife his father took had been smashed crockery, anguished wailing and screaming threats—even years after she had left him and taken Cyrus with her.

Until this moment, he had not understood that he wanted that from Hope. And that what he wanted from this woman was some kind of indication that she—

But he stopped himself. That she…what?

Cared about him?

When he knew very well she did not. When he should not want her to in the first place. Nothing about this had anything to do with *caring*.

One of the things Cyrus had long enjoyed about his life and his position was the clarity of purpose it provided. He knew what his job was. He knew how he was meant to rule.

Cyrus had known exactly who he was since he was an adolescent.

His father had made sure that the things that were expected of Cyrus were etched deep into his bones.

He did not like this murkiness. He despised the way it sat upon him, a mess of something too dark and far too edgy for comfort.

And this woman dared to sit there *beaming* at him,

as if he had offered her gifts instead of the kind of marriage she was supposed to find horrible.

"You wish to choose your own rivals?" He made himself laugh. "Let me guess. You think you can rule over them that way."

It was proper protocol to wait for the monarch to take his seat and taste his food before anyone else dared, but naturally Hope did as she liked. She broke off a piece of flatbread from one of the platters arrayed before her, then dipped it into a bowl of hummus flavored with garlic and tahini. She popped the bite into her mouth and closed her eyes for a moment, another example of that sensuality of hers and the way it infused everything.

The way it infused *him*.

It made his entire body clench tight.

And he wanted to believe that she did this deliberately to toy with him—but he could not quite make himself accept that. Hope seemed too unselfconscious. As if she didn't much care if he stood before her, watching her, or not.

He could not understand why that made his hunger for her all the more intense.

When she opened her eyes again, her golden gaze looked merry. "I don't believe that these women would be rivals at all." His disbelief must have showed on his face because she smiled. "It sounds like fun. Built-in friends and no one has to feel as if they do too much of anything. All of the labor is shared. Isn't that the point?"

"That is not the point." He folded his arms over his chest. "A man shows his wealth and might to the kingdom by the number of wives he is able to support. And then again, by the number of sons he has."

"So a mighty fortress and calling yourself King of this and Lord of that doesn't do the trick, then?"

"I tire of these games of yours," he gritted out.

But he was not tired. And she did not look at all chastened.

So Cyrus lowered himself to the cushions, and lay back. Then he waved a peremptory hand before him. "I think it is time you dance for me, wife. As is only fitting."

She went still, her hand hovering over the flatbread. For moment, he thought she might balk.

Did he want her to? Was that the point of this?

But in the next moment, she smiled. "I would love to, but I'm terrible. The women have been wonderful teachers and everyone agrees that while I'll never be up to the standard of a girl who's been doing these dances since birth, I should be competent enough in time, and potentially less embarrassing, too."

"Dance," he told her, gruffly. "Do not speak."

He knew as the words left his mouth that he wanted her to argue. Because he already regretted asking for this. Because when she moved, the silk moved with her, like a man's caress.

And when she got all the way to her feet and stood before him, there was no pretending that his hunger for her wasn't taking him over. It was.

There was no pretending that there was anything cold or calculating about this.

He was so hungry for her it nearly hurt.

"I still think it's weird that there's no music for this," she told him, when he could hear nothing but music in his own head.

He shook his head, but the music kept on. "Dance anyway."

She laughed a little, under her breath. But then she began.

And perhaps Cyrus had intended for this to snap him out of the spell he seemed to be under where she was concerned.

Perhaps he had thought that alone, without the other women to surround her and encourage her, she would be nothing but awkward and lose some of that brashness he found so baffling.

Perhaps that was what he wanted.

But instead, this woman he had taken to wife and had only kissed the slightest bit for his trouble, closed her eyes.

The way she did when she intended to enjoy something to the full, God help him.

And slowly, she began to roll her hips this way and that, making the silk dance around her.

That age-old song of his people. That call to lust and longing.

With that same sensuality that he saw in everything she did, Hope danced like fire, like flame.

Her feet were bare against the floor. He could see the enticing length of her legs nearly all the way up to her thighs, depending on how the silks moved. He could see most of her belly, jewels winking in her navel. And the top she wore looked soft and gleamed as she swayed, picking up the light in the room.

As she danced, she tipped her head back, a smile on her lips as if she was as lost in the pleasure of this as much as he was.

Maybe more.

It was too much.

"Open your eyes," he ordered her, in a gravelly voice he could not seem to control. "Dance for your king." She lowered her head, still moving, and opened up her eyes as he'd commanded. But that meant he was caught by all that gold. And revealed by it in turn, for he could not keep himself from gritting out what he shouldn't. "Dance for your husband, Hope."

And then everything was flame.

Everything was the roll of her hips, the fire in her molten gold eyes.

She danced and she danced, until they were both breathing too quickly. Still she kept on, whirling around and around the room, until Cyrus couldn't tell if she was claiming it, or him.

Or if she already had.

Maybe that was what pushed him to stand and go to her, sweeping her up into his arms, then carrying her across the vast chamber to his bed.

At last.

"I want your kisses," he told her, feeling rough and outside himself and as if he might perish if he did not do something about this madness clamoring inside him, this abominable need he could neither quit nor ignore. "But tonight, *omri*, I do not want you to stop."

She looked too beautiful there, finally lying in his arms. Her cheeks were flushed and her eyes were bright. Her golden hair fell all around her.

And she could not seem to lie still, as if the dance claimed her still.

As if she wanted to test out that same age-old rhythm with him, in the time-honored fashion.

Hope took a steadying sort of breath, and when she smiled he was sure he saw a wickedness there. It called to things in him he would have said could not possibly exist.

For Cyrus had been raised hard. His duties and responsibilities had been hammered into him again and again and again. He was the Lord of the desert and he did not bend, he did not break. He did not deviate from his path, and woe betide any who dared stand against him.

Even in song inside his own head.

But they were not standing, Hope and him.

And her smile made him wonder if he knew himself at all.

“I won’t stop if you won’t,” she said, and it was a challenge. A dare.

And then she pressed her lips to his, rocked her hips against him, and Cyrus forgot he was anything but this.

Flesh and blood and a man.

And hers, whether he liked it or not.

CHAPTER EIGHT

SENSATION WAS LIKE the music for dancing that Hope quickly found she didn't miss.

This melody was heat and flame.

It was the way Cyrus used his hands, his palms creating their own symphony against her skin.

And now they were wrapped around each other on this bed that had loomed so large in her imagination since the day she'd arrived in this fortress of stone, a monument against the sand.

How many times had she dreamed about the things they might do here? How many nights had she lain in her bed in the harem, pretending her own hands belonged to him instead? Now she wasn't pretending. Now it was finally happening.

And it put all her dreams to shame.

Cyrus was made of that same perfect bronze, everywhere. And as he held himself above her, the harsh lines of his face did not soften, precisely, but there was something about the intense way he gazed down at her that made her feel as if she did the softening for him.

Especially when his mouth was a stark line that

carved out a hollow space within her, a cavern of fire and longing.

She was not at all surprised at the way she ached for him even now, with that melting heat everywhere. That ache was inside her, an overwhelming wildness that felt not unlike the desert outside. Shifting, voracious. An expanse with no end. Beautiful and terrible and all-consuming.

But then, he was the same.

Cyrus took her wrists in his hand, hauling her arms up over her head so that her breasts jutted up against him.

She had spent too long his harem, perhaps. Because she liked the way her breasts performed for him. For that look on his harshly beautiful face. For the way his dark eyes gleamed as he looked down upon her, freeing her quickly from the silk that barely contained the bounty that was his.

Only his.

The way her nipples were bold and needy and jutted toward him pleased her. Just as dancing for him had pleased her.

Because kissing this man had not broken any spells. If anything, kissing him had cast new ones, spinning her out and into the endless enchantment of need and desire, so she felt lost somewhere in the magic.

But the kind of lost that felt a whole lot like finding herself at last.

Especially when Cyrus made a low, deep noise of purely male approval at the sight of her breasts unbound for him.

He bent, one hand flat on the mattress beside her and the other stretched high to hold her hands where he wanted them, and he took one nipple deep into his mouth.

And as far as Hope could tell, tossed her straight into that molten flame.

Especially when Cyrus settled in as if he planned to be there some while.

Then he set himself to the task of driving her mad.

First he used his tongue and the suction of his devilish mouth. Then he used the edge of his teeth. As she arched against him, desperate to give him more—and more still—he slid his hands down to span her ribs so he might hold her up to him like an offering.

His mouth was a glorious delirium, and then he would use one hand to make the sensation that much more intense. That much better.

Over and over again, and all Hope could do was surrender.

To the crash of lightning, one strike after the next. To the wild storm of passion that taught her things about herself she hadn't known before. Like the way everything was connected. That there was a straight line from each breast down into her core, and he knew precisely how to play it to make her moan.

He knew exactly how to make her little more than his instrument. How to play her body expertly until she was sobbing and shaking.

And then, even better, hurtled straight off the side of the cliff he'd made and broke apart entirely in midair.

For a while, then—perhaps an eternity—she drifted off somewhere. Into the starry night itself.

But she floated her way back down to earth, and she found that Cyrus had gone to the trouble of removing his clothes and was even now dispensing with what remained of hers.

And when he slid back into place beside her, the feel of his naked skin against hers was sweet and hot and so perfect she thought she might cry.

Everything inside her was humming and yielding, like she was made of honey, and she wanted nothing more than to sink into it. To *become* it.

Meanwhile, everything about Cyrus seemed heavy and taut and almost too hot, and that felt like more evidence that all of this was *right.*

That despite the distraction of harem dances and her daily calls to a surprisingly not distraught Mignon, *this* was the point. That it didn't matter how she'd gotten here or what had come before. That she could have conducted a thousand not-quite dates with appalling men, and none of them mattered at all, because her whole life had been leading to this.

To him.

To *now.*

"Cyrus…" she began, in a voice that sounded both like her and not like her at all.

As if she was already changed forever.

"Quiet, *omri,*" he murmured. His gaze was a glittering thing and she wasn't sure what left more fire in its wake—the places where his eyes traveled or the work of his hands. Either way, she could feel that softness in her shifting already, heating up, becoming its own bright heat. "The time for words has passed."

And that seemed more than fine to Hope, because words took effort and all she wanted to do was throw herself headfirst—again—into the abandonment he promised with every touch, every look.

A promise he had already more than kept.

But first Cyrus took it upon himself to explore every bit of her body.

He flipped her so that she was facedown on the bed and she found herself laughing with the sheer joy of it as he began at her feet, then took his time, seeming to learn every bit of her while she pressed herself into the caress of the sheets beneath her and felt her own temperature skyrocket.

And by the time he made it to her neck, she wasn't laughing any longer.

He pressed hot, stirring kisses to her nape. And his hands were like angels and demons at once, making her writhe and moan.

Cyrus held her to him, palming the side of her face and turning her head so that his mouth could find hers.

His kiss was bold and deep, demanding and stirring, and she could do nothing but give herself over to it—to him—completely.

Especially when he took his other hand and stroked his way over one breast, down to her navel, and then, at last, found her soft, swollen folds.

He played there for a moment, then delved within.

It was almost too much, Hope thought, but she could barely form the ghost of that thought in her own head.

Because he drew figure eights in her softness, learning the honeyed contours of her most secret place. And even as she moaned into his mouth, his tongue stroked her there, too.

And when she shuddered at the dual assault, his fingers reached deeper and he found her entrance.

Then, with an inexorable twist of his wrist, he thrust a long, hard finger in deep.

Making everything seemed to throb and glow.

He kissed her and kissed her, still holding her splayed out between his mouth and his hand.

At her core, he played her expertly, that impossibly hard finger inside her while his thumb found her proud center, making her buck against him, moving her hips in an inexpert haze of joy and need—

Until she broke apart all over again.

And this time, Cyrus didn't let her drift off.

He rolled her over to her back, and found his way between her legs, drawing them open and settling himself between them.

Hope was still sobbing wildly, still shaking.

And that hard jut of his manhood that she had felt against the small of her back became something else again as he ran the length of it through her folds, making the storm that gripped her go on and on and on.

Making her shake even more at the size of him.

And the sure knowledge that he intended to replace his finger with...*that.*

Hope might have been a virgin, but there was nothing shy about her.

Quite the opposite. She'd researched. Extensively.

From films so explicit she'd had to watch them from between her fingers to breathtaking erotic writing that had made her a little too susceptible to unfortunate fantasies that she knew better than to hope the sort of man she was set to marry might fulfill in some way. Much less exceed.

She knew where all the parts went and how they fit together. She had done her level best to get ready so that nothing would faze her too badly no matter who she ended up marrying.

But nothing could have prepared her for Cyrus. Or how this *felt.*

When Cyrus lowered his hard, beautiful chest to hers. When he wrapped his arms around her, holding her so much closer, so much tighter than she had imagined—because, something in her understood belatedly, all the films she'd watched had been staged for a viewer.

Here, now, there were only the two of them.

The two of them and this magic conflagration between them.

The two of them and too much sensation to bear in one body. Maybe that was why it took two in the first place, to share the glory between them, because surely it would otherwise be too much.

Especially because he knew how to wield that great, hard, and hot part of him that he rubbed and rubbed through her softness, driving her mad.

Making her feel turned inside out.

And all of that was nothing—a clamoring whirlwind of a glorious nothing—next to how it felt when he reached down between them, wrapped his fist around his thickness, and guided himself to her molten channel at last.

His finger had felt too big, a decidedly male intrusion, but this was something else again.

This was an undoing.

Cyrus pressed his way in, but only slightly, stopping when both of them felt him catch on the flesh that his finger had eased past, but the enormity of his manhood could not.

His midnight gaze found hers, and she could not tell which one of them was breathing heavier just then. Nor which one of them was making that sound, so raw, so needy, that seemed to fill her from within.

He did not speak. She could not have answered.

And still, it was as if a whole conversation happened there in that lightning hit of his gaze to hers.

Some understanding. Some knowledge, primitive though it might have been.

A kind of anguish on his face that even here, even now, she had succeeded in surprising him.

Something entirely feminine and deeply held within her seemed to nod, as if she'd known how this would be all along.

As if she'd known it would be him, and now, and *this* since before she'd known her own name.

"Forgive me, *omri*," Cyrus murmured, and his voice was like a dark ribbon of sound that tied itself around her. And with her thighs wide open to hold him and all of him pressed between them, he had finally said those words as if he meant them.

My life. Forgive me.

It didn't occur to her to ask him why he needed her forgiveness, or to tell him it was already freely given, or to wonder why this moment felt like an intense *recognition*—

Instead he thrust home.

And everything went dark.

Then burst into light, so bright and so hot that Hope wasn't sure she could tell the difference between a marvelous pain and a maddening pleasure.

It was so *intense*. It was too much, of everything. He was too big, and she *couldn't*, and she could hear, far off in the distance, sounds she knew were her own odd little pants—

But Hope couldn't possibly care about that, because he pulled back out a little, then thrust deep again.

Making room.

Making a kind of symphony tear through her, like a new kind of storm.

And then, stroke by stroke, Cyrus taught her how to sing.

With every part of her body.

He taught her what it was to be a song. How the two of them fit together, wrapped tight around each other, melody and descant at once.

He taught her how to climb straight up to a high note so pure, so good, it felt like flying.

And how to fall, brought back to earth with each ruthless thrust of him inside her.

Again and again and again, they sang this song. They learned the words. She tasted them on his tongue. She dug her fingers into his wide back, and learned a far better dance with her hips against his.

Until, at last, she felt apart so hard it made her voice shake.

Cyrus followed her, shouting out his pleasure.

Then he wrapped her in his arms, murmuring words in his language that made her shiver all the more, and let them both go still.

Hope thought lifetimes might have passed. He rolled over, taking his weight from her and pulling her with him. She lay splayed out over his chest, her ear over his heart, and found she could hardly remember a *before* or think about an *after*.

There was only that drumbeat beneath her. The heat of his skin. Cyrus, all around her, and his hair-roughened thighs against hers to remind her even now of their differences. Of his delicious maleness that she wanted to explore all over again.

Just as soon as she caught her breath.

She thought he would hate it if he knew that she could hear his heartbeat. If he knew how deeply that pleased her. How she wanted to dance to the beat of that low thunder beneath her head.

Eventually she felt his hand as he moved it up and down the length of her spine, easily. Lazily.

Spinning out a new, sweet flame as it went.

And when she shifted to look up at him, his midnight gaze seemed brighter than usual, almost as if—

But he was moving before she could complete that thought, bringing her with him. He swept her up into his arms and this time, did not toss her over his shoulder as he had in that chapel she could barely recall.

This time he held her before him, so she could have laid her head on his shoulder if she wished. He carried her through the mazelike rooms of his apartments, down yet another stone stair, until they ended up in a place she knew well. The baths.

Except these were not the harem baths, tucked away where the hot springs bubbled from below, hidden away in the belly of the fortress. He walked her past a long pool with windows than arched up over the central courtyard that would have let the light in, if it were day. He carried her up a set of wide, mosaic-laid stairs, and then into what seemed like its own oasis.

There were smaller pools gathered here and there beneath clusters of trees, and up above, when she tipped her head back, she realized she could see the stars.

Cyrus took her over to the furthest pool that bubbled and murmured into the night. He did not release his hold on her as he stepped in, then settled them both on the bench beneath the water.

Hope sighed a little as the warm water enveloped her, assuming he would let go of her. Set her aside now that they were both wet.

But instead he shifted how he held her, and kept her in his lap, her back to his chest and his chin resting on the top of her head.

And between the heat of the pool and the hard heat of his body, she felt sleepy. Yet wide awake. Because she felt far more safe and secure than perhaps she should have.

Not like a child. Not like that little girl that she had been in her papa's study, but as if this had been the point all along. To grow up, leave home, and find a place or person that could make her feel as gloriously alive and as much of a woman as he had tonight, but then also give her this besides.

As if, at last, she was protected. The way her father had intended.

Hope felt her heart kick at her, hard, at the thought.

It was like this intimacy with Cyrus bled into everything. As if, even now, sitting in this water, she was changing.

His fingers played idly with her hair, his body was a warm, slick chair, and the water was like a soft prayer all around them. She didn't want to say a word. She didn't want to think.

Hope wanted nothing more than this.

For as long as *this* might last.

And, unbidden, she felt a well of understanding for her sweet, silly mother wash over her then, there in the starlight. Was this what Mignon had always been after? This sense that she was finally complete?

Because Hope was tempted to believe that nothing truly bad could ever happen when there was this connection, this quiet joy.

That this was the beginning and the end of everything.

"You should have told me," Cyrus said some long while later, there in the quiet dark, lit only by the stars far above. "You should have told me from the first."

She didn't pretend not to understand what he meant. "Would you have believed me if I had?"

Hope felt more than heard him sigh at that. And then his hands were on her, shifting her around so that she knelt up over him, there in the thick, soft water.

Hope's eyes had long since adjusted to the dark. And sitting this way was better, because that bronze face of his was covered in stars and it was as if all of that shine blurred the sharp, cruelly beautiful edges.

So that he looked the way he always did when she imagined him, alone in her bed.

She followed an urge she might have restrained in the daytime, tracing the shape of his cheekbones and then that stark, hard line of his mouth.

"You should have told me," he said again, but his voice was darker then.

Hope thought it sounded more like a condemnation of himself than of her.

"If I'm honest," she told him, "I quite preferred the moral high ground."

She'd meant that to lighten the mood, somehow. She even smiled, but he only looked at her as if she was some kind of ghost.

"As well you should," he told her then, in that voice of his that sounded like a proclamation. "But I have always held myself to higher standards of behavior than others. When I am wrong I say it, and I have wronged you, *omri*."

And then there was nothing light in Hope, either. Only the weight of his gaze and the way he looked at her, straight on, so there could be no hiding from this. From the apology he made so fully and matter-of-factly.

"Allow me to compensate you for any suffering I might have caused," he said in a low voice. "An apology, if you will."

"I don't want your apologies," she told him, though she would treasure his all the same. I want—"

"Hope." And she stilled as he held her there, still kneeling over him. "I know what you want, if nothing else."

And she thought she should argue about that, but he was huge and hard between them and she was already shivery with delight.

Then his hands were on her bottom, shifting her up and over him, so he could work his way inside her, slick and hot. Until he was settled in deep, nudging the very depths of her once more.

Where he stayed, his gaze as hard on her as he was deep inside her, watching her work to accommodate him. Because he filled her so completely and slightly more than was comfortable.

And she had never imagined that he could feel like this. It was as if she had never been more herself than when he was deep inside her, connecting them like this. Changing everything.

Changing her most of all.

And Hope didn't need him to tell her what to do, just like she didn't need all of that research she had done before. Her mind was a perfect blank of everything but this.

There was nothing for her but him.

Nothing but Cyrus, forever.

And then her body's insistence that she roll her hips and teach herself how to rock back and forth against that deep shaft of pure male fire deep inside.

She did it again and again.

And it was different like this, kneeling over him and rubbing the greediest part of her against him every time she moved.

It was different this time, because she knew where they were going. Because she had an inkling, now, of the catastrophic joy that awaited them both.

Because you love him, came a voice from deep inside her that sounded too much like fate, like another thing she had always known—

But she threw that aside, because what mattered was this, him, now.

This apology of his that felt like grace. Like a new song and the same song, blended into one, into *them.*

What mattered was the sensation, nothing more.

Because he might have made her his wife, but Hope knew full well that she was still his captive.

And love had nothing to do with this.

So she told herself as she rode them both to a shattering finish, and poured herself out into his hands.

Again and again and again.

CHAPTER NINE

HOPE'S VIRGINITY WAS yet another shock this woman had delivered to him.

It was the biggest yet.

Cyrus could admit, days later, that he still had not fully taken that particular reality on board.

Because he had misjudged her. He had wronged her, as he had said. And he could take all his men to task for failing him—he did—but that didn't change the broader issue. Cyrus, who prided himself on his discernment, had been completely and utterly wrong about the woman he'd married.

In every respect.

He didn't know what to *do* with that. He didn't know what it *meant*.

What else was he wrong about? What else had he missed?

These questions haunted him.

And having enjoyed her in full at last, he had spent the whole next day doing nothing but exulting in her, certain he would find himself satiated at any moment. But when that moment never arrived—because, once again, he was entirely wrong—he thought it prudent to institute some rules.

Meaning, it became a necessity.

Because he was the King. He was the Lord of this desert and he could not lose himself in a woman's bed, no matter how tempting Hope was to him.

So he waited with ill-concealed and somewhat worrying eagerness until nightfall each day, when he could meet with her at last, suffer through a meal, and then gorge himself on what he truly wanted.

Tonight, while Hope licked her fingers and drove him mad with her greedy little noises in appreciation of the sweet pastries she claimed were her favorite, he thought he might as well satisfy his curiosity as well as his other, baser urges.

If gracelessly. "I don't understand why you made it seem as if you had enjoyed the company of so many men when you had not done anything of the kind," he said, as if she was to blame for the reports his men had delivered to him and the conclusions he had reached.

"I don't know what made you think I was enjoying the company of men in the first place," Hope replied in her usual bright and carefree way, here in the privacy of the tower, where their only ceiling was the starry night high above.

She lounged back against the bright pillows, and no longer did the silks she wore seem like a costume. It was clear to him that she inhabited them fully. That somehow, she had become the very height of femininity to him, awash in wiles and without peer.

Or maybe it was simply that he knew too well how happy he was to watch the silk against her skin, caressing her as he knew he would. And soon.

He told himself restraint was a virtue, though at the moment it felt far more like a curse.

And he knew too well now that she was not the brazen, careless, hedonistic socialite he'd imagined her before he'd met her. No morally bankrupt creature like so many he had met while doing his Oxbridge duty and had assumed she emulated.

There was also that part of him that knew too well that he had already felt lost in her long before he knew of her innocence. He had already wanted her too much.

He had already married her and had already been entirely too consumed with kissing her—but he did not choose to focus on those uncomfortable truths. Not now.

He frowned at her instead. "I still cannot understand what you thought you were doing. Surely there were better options available to you than looking for a potential husband in such an unseemly way."

She eyed him lazily, almost insolently, from her pillows. "How did you set about looking for a wife?" she asked. "I was under the impression your grandmother made arrangements and you signed papers, sight unseen. Would that have been better? More *seemly*, somehow, than going out to dinner the way people have been doing for ages?"

He regretted telling her the details of how the contract she'd never seen had come to be, not that he planned to admit such a thing. Because Cyrus had the lowering suspicion that once he started making more admissions, the fortress would crumble all around him like so much dust.

And he wasn't sure if he meant the actual fortress they sat in or…himself.

"Better than letting it look as if you were dating half the men in London? Yes."

"It only looked that way if you were spying on me when you could have helped me," she said reprovingly, though her eyes were gleaming. "But even if I had been dating merrily, so what? That's another thing people do, you know."

And he knew the cheeky look she got about her when she was poking at him, deliberately, because he usually answered in the way that pleased them both the most. Cyrus could not say he minded it.

Still, today, he ignored his body's immediate reaction to that sparkle in her gaze. "People might," he agreed. "But not you. Not an innocent who hardly knew what her body was for when I met her."

He stated that as fact. And knew it was one when she flushed.

"I know what my body is for now," she said, her voice soft.

Cyrus no longer sat across from her, because that was too far away after whole days apart. And because if there was a table between them, he could not do what he did now and simply pull her close so he could get his mouth on her. So he could pull her over him, or beneath him, or like now, simply flush against the side of his body, because he always preferred to feel her.

"Hope." He said her name, there against her mouth. "Why?"

She breathed something that sounded like his name, and then she sat back, pushing her golden hair back as she moved. And there was something almost helpless in her bright gaze when she looked at him. "My mother."

"Your mother made you date these men?" he asked, astonished—and instantly deciding to cut the older woman off entirely.

"Of course not." Hope sat back from him, and frowned down at the place where her hands rested on her own thighs as she knelt there beside him. "She would have loved to save us herself. She tried. Oh, how she tried. But she wasn't made for hard things."

"Softness is an indulgence," Cyrus told her, not sure why his chest felt tight. "If you do not indulge it, it cannot rule you."

"And a dandelion is unlikely to turn into a loaded gun simply because it stops coddling itself," Hope replied, with a laugh. But the laugh ended quickly, and now she was looking at him with that helpless gaze that made that tightness in his chest…worse. "But I wasn't made to be a pretty flower. It made sense that it was me."

"You were the child." Cyrus scowled at her. "It was her responsibility to care for you, not the other way around."

And he heard himself say that. He heard it, and he

felt it, too. The way it made his own bones seem to shift their places inside him.

Worse, he saw that helpless look on Hope's face shift too, into something like compassion. "If she could have, she would have. But I love her too, you see. So I did what needed doing and regretted that I couldn't do more. That there were…limits to what I could stomach doing. She didn't hold that against me. She isn't like that. She's like a hummingbird, dancing from one sweet thing to the next. That's where she's best."

"She should have tried parenting," Cyrus said, because he couldn't seem to stop. Not even when the words made his bones feel as if they were breaking themselves inside him. Not even when he couldn't decide if he was betraying the memory of the man who'd made him or finally speaking the one terrible truth he'd been avoiding since he'd been brought to this place when he was twelve.

But if he chose, if he acknowledged what this was, he didn't know what would happen to him. He didn't know what would become of him.

If so many of the pillars he'd built his life on were wrong, if *he* was wrong, then who was he?

And somehow, Hope seemed to know that, too. Because she leaned in and slid her hand over his jaw. "I don't hold that against her, either. Do you know why?"

Cyrus was terribly afraid he did.

But he couldn't seem to stop her from saying it anyway. He couldn't seem to move.

"Because that's what love is," Hope told him with a quiet certainty and that look in her eyes. "It forgives and loves on, no matter what. There's nothing soft about that."

And Cyrus wanted to shout his own battlements down, but he could not let himself do such things. He was the King.

So instead he hauled her to him. And then he showed her precisely how he felt about the things she'd said to him tonight, right there on the tower floor, bathing them both in starlight, as if that could chase away that ache in his bones.

As if that could hold off the storm Cyrus was terrified was coming for him, no matter how clear the skies looked as the sands shifted all around him. Whispering of a reckoning to come.

Whispering words he had never allowed to be spoken in his hearing.

Singing old songs he kept imagining he could scrub from his mind entirely, only to wake up with those same old melodies on his tongue.

More days passed, turning into weeks. Summer settled in. And even though Cyrus knew it was long past time that he got back to his usual travels, staying in each of the desert's four separate regions for a season so that his people could know him and follow him because they knew he understood them, too—he was loathe to do it.

Just as he found himself curiously uninterested in adding to his harem as originally planned. No matter how many times his man discreetly placed the tablet back in the center of his desk, he set it aside and focused on other matters.

He told himself he was merely indulging this strange

desire for Hope that had overtaken him, but that he would soon grow bored. For nothing could last, this he knew. That was one of the desert's finest lessons. Nothing was truly permanent, save change itself.

Certainly nothing this intense, this all-consuming.

Storms were not made for longevity. His father had taught him that long ago, right here in the fortress. They had watched sandstorms—sometimes from the safety of these walls and sometimes out in them with only a makeshift cave for shelter—and no matter how terrifying, they always blew themselves out. And no matter the new formations, the dunes knocked down here and raised again there, it was still the desert.

The desert always remained.

And so too would Cyrus once this particular storm blew itself out.

He held on to that.

He told himself that it was no catastrophe that all he thought about was Hope. It was simply the nature of a storm—who thought of other things while sand whirled about like rain? So too during all of his calls, all of his tedious video conferences, all the short trips that felt like an imposition instead of a part of his sworn duty—he found that he could not give the whole of his attention as he usually did because part of it was always with her.

The summer wore on and he told himself that even though this madness between them seemed to grow in intensity by the day, it would stop. It would end.

As all things ended.

But in the meantime, he was like a man possessed.

It didn't matter how many times he told himself that

she was only a woman, and surely no woman was that much different from another.

Because it seemed to him in those hours when he moved inside of her—when they came together again and again so that it seemed there was no end or beginning to the shapes they made or the things they felt—he knew deep inside of him that if asked, he would be unable to remember if he had ever touched another.

He could hardly remember it away from her, either.

One night, while waiting for his guards to bring her to him so they could enact that formal handoff that he knew pleased them both with its archaic formality, he found himself thinking that all his ancestors who'd stood here before him were to be pitied. For surely none of them had found a woman like this. A woman like Hope. If they had, he knew, there would have been no need for a harem in the first place.

But even as he thought such a thing, it infuriated him.

Or rather, what infuriated him was that he thought the notion ought to enrage him—but it didn't.

As if his particular storm was here to stay.

And when he heard her feet behind him, he was scowling as he turned to look at her.

She did not pause. Not Hope. She came straight to him anyway, her fingers finding that furrow between his brows and smoothing it away.

More damning, he let her.

"Do I displease you tonight?" she asked, but not as if she had the slightest worry that she might. "It's my dancing, isn't it? You've finally accepted what I told you all along. I really am utterly dreadful."

Cyrus should have hated that she made him want to laugh. But he didn't hate it. He didn't hate a single thing about her and that was the trouble. He could even feel his mouth betray him with the slightest curve.

It was an outrage.

"You are truly dreadful," he agreed, but he found that outrage couldn't quite take hold. "But I like it."

He could not wait for the ritual of a meal. He took her then in a swift glut of what he told himself was fury, tossing her over the edge of the bed and kicking her legs aside. He tugged her silks out of his way so he could slam himself inside her, lifting her hips up to meet him as he took her in a hurry from behind.

As if he thought that if he gave himself over to the madness of it all, she would not join him in the glorious, plummeting fall from such heights. That if she didn't, that might put him right at last.

But she did. She always did.

Even if, like tonight, she dared to reach down herself and make certain of it.

No other woman would dare, Cyrus knew. No other woman would dream of taking pleasure he didn't give her. It would be seen as an insult.

He did not understand why it was that he loved it when this one did as she pleased.

Cyrus could not even manage to pretend to feel it as some kind of insult, because he liked it when she shattered all around him, her tight sheath gripping him, tugging him, taking him with her when she took flight.

Later, after they'd showered together—and he'd spent some time using her sweetness an appetizer, kneeling before her as the water beat down and licking that sweet honey from between her legs that he found he craved far more than anything served from his kitchens—they settled in for a meal before the windows that let in the desert.

It was starting to get darker sooner. It was full dark now, when, back when he'd first brought her here, they had watched the last of the sunset over their meals.

Cyrus had to acknowledge that the coming change of seasons made him restless. As if the turning of the earth would force him into making the decisions he been putting off, if not facing the storms he knew were coming for him.

"If I am your wife because you said so when we arrived, does that make me your queen as well?" Hope asked, drawing his attention back to her from the great desert outside.

Another woman would have asked that question in a voice filled with court intrigue and politics, but this was Hope. She seemed far more focused on the savory dishes in pots before her. He could not imagine that she was suddenly showing any real interest in the Aminabad throne.

Perhaps that was why it seemed no particular hardship to answer her in a way he would not have done if he'd imagined she was angling for a crown, like too many of the women he'd met in his lifetime—blurry as they all seemed to him now.

"They are not the same," he told her. "In order to

be known as my queen, I would need to pronounce you such. My father was renowned for having many queens, one after the next. It was a gift he gave each new wife when he thought they might be the one to give him another son. It was not a gift he ever extended to my mother."

"Because he was punishing her." And it was only when he had been silent some while, glaring at her, that Hope looked up. She blinked, looking baffled. "Did I say something wrong?"

"My mother kidnapped the heir to this kingdom, Hope. You seem to forget that."

"Yes, but he kidnapped you right back. If it was wrong when she did it, why was it right when he did it in return?"

Her eyes were clear gold and there was no reason he should feel as if they pierced him straight through.

"The issue of whether or not she was a queen was before all of that," he heard himself say.

Hope tilted her head to one side, holding a piece of the flatbread she preferred in her fingers. "But she'd already given him a son. You."

And it struck without warning, the storm he'd been hoping he might avoid after all. The last remaining pillar seemed to crumble into dust between them, and without the howl and thunder he had been expecting.

It was such a quiet thing, in the end.

His father had punished his mother after she'd given him a son, but before she'd taken Cyrus away from him. He had refused to make her his queen. The scenes that Cyrus remembered, of shouting and weeping and smashing crockery, must have occurred between those two things, though his father had always made it sound as if his treatment of Cyrus's mother was predicated entirely on her betrayal.

But what if that wasn't the truth? What if the things his father had always told him were as wrong as everything else?

What if it had all been a lie for a cruel man to not only justify his treatment of his wife, but of his son?

What if Cyrus's entire life was the lie?

He felt the floor beneath him seem to buckle. He focused on the frown on Hope's lovely face.

"You are not my queen," he told her, as if it was a confession. His voice felt gritty in his own mouth. "Unless I choose to make you my queen. The kingdom is always mine—you would be Queen only at my pleasure."

And he understood as he said it that this, too, was a cruelty his father had visited first upon his mother, then upon him. He had given every other wife the designation, purely to rub salt in the wound. But then, after beating it into Cyrus that he was to hate the woman who had stolen him from a man Cyrus knew full well was barbaric, he had seen to it that Cyrus would repeat the cycle.

"It is easy to take a wife," he made himself say, because she was still watching him, still frowning at him, as if she sensed the storm yet could not see it. "It is slightly more complicated to make that wife a queen, as it requires more people. So yes, there is a ceremony of sorts. The woman in question does not need to be present, though she can be. It is typically a conversation between a king and his men, asking them to offer fealty to the new Queen."

"Naturally." Hope eyed him. "Why should the woman be involved at all? You might as well make the nearest chair your queen, by that logic."

He was surprised that hadn't been suggested. Instead, his father had seen to it that Cyrus would marry an Englishwoman because it was tradition and hate her, too, because he'd spent so many years being primed to find her every move suspect. It would not surprise him in the least if the old King was somehow responsible for that missing contract, too.

If he had somehow made certain that Cyrus would come into his marriage filled with exactly the sort of deep, cruel fury his father had claimed was a family trait.

Cyrus had always seen himself as more rational than his father, though he had wisely kept that to himself. He had always assumed that when tested, he would never behave as the old man had.

And yet he had kidnapped this woman with his own two hands. He had thrown her over his shoulder and carried her away, and it was only by the greatest luck—luck he did not deserve—that she happened to be *this* woman, who had laughed in his face, danced in his harem, and ruined him completely.

But the nights were growing colder. It was impossible to pretend that summer was not coming to a close. A whole season that he had spent here, with her, instead of doing what he had long held to be the most critical part of his duty.

He knew that was on him.

Just as he knew that he could not be around this woman again until he looked himself full in the mirror and undertook his own reckoning.

Until he found out who he really was, not simply who his father had made him.

"It is unacceptable that the Lord of the Aminabad Desert should be beholden to anyone," he decreed then, making her eyes go wide. "Much less a woman. You must see that this can't go on, Hope. Not like this. It is time to return to reality."

"It was the talk of queens, wasn't it," Hope said, staring back at him. Though she didn't look at all concerned. "It wound you right up."

"I am not *wound up*." But he wasn't going to argue with her. He was going to do what he should have done a long time ago and act like the King he'd been born to be, not the man who had been made in the fire of old cruelties and too many poisons to name. "I will leave you here. You can carry on as you like. You might even get the hang of dancing."

"Dancing," she repeated, as if he'd said something shocking.

"I will return to you next summer," he told her and this time, he meant it as the decree it was. "My men will let me know how you are faring."

"Oh, good," Hope said, though her eyes were dark. "They've always been so good at that."

"We had a summer," he said, though he was afraid he could feel his own body crumbling where he stood. As if he was one more pillar rendered unto dust by these terrible truths he still didn't want to face. But he would. "We will have another one."

It felt like a concession. Yet as his words hung there in the bedchamber between them, Cyrus reflected on the fact that, really, he could have chosen his moment with more care.

This announcement would likely have gone over better if he had not been seized with his usual hunger for her when she'd arrived tonight. If he had not blurted it out like that.

If he could find a way to stop looking at her as if she was the only safety from the storm he'd ever known while she looked at him as if he'd taken leave of his senses.

Still, he had not expected her laughter.

Particularly because it did not sound the way it normally did.

Tonight he thought it seemed tinged with a little bit of that hysteria that he remembered from long ago.

He found he liked it a lot less now.

"That sounds like a great plan." Hope did not sound as if she thought it sounded anything like great. But she was smoothing her silks back into place, so only the way her hair swung indicated that she was more agitated than she wished to show him. "There are only two problems, as far as I can see."

He stepped away from her, because he could not seem to think straight when she was near. "There are no problems. It will go as I have said it will. For so I have decreed it."

"You can decree it all you like," Hope said, her voice

more clipped than he was used to hearing it. Even the gold of her gaze looked far darker. "Your first problem, though I'm sure you'll consider it a minor and inconsequential one, is that I'm in love with you, Cyrus. For my sins."

"That is nothing to do with me," he growled out at her, because it should have been exactly that. Nothing. Air. Forgotten as soon as it was said.

He certainly shouldn't feel a kind of roaring triumph deep within him. This was what he had wanted at the start though he had nearly forgotten it, somehow, over the course of these months. She was *meant* to be in love with him.

This was the whole point. He'd wanted her to feel sick with it. To suffer for it.

He had always assumed that when she told him it had happened, as it inevitably would, he would laugh. Because his revenge would be complete.

Tonight, he did not feel like laughing.

Because if he did, wouldn't that mean it was his father's revenge that had won the day? It would mean he had made Cyrus exactly like him. The kind of man who would take a woman away from everything she knew, love her until she loved him back, then tell her it had all been a bit of seduction and he would never feel the same.

Wasn't that the trajectory of his parents' relationship?

How could he ever have imagined he could behave this way? Cyrus couldn't access the man of fury who had so coldly told this woman that he would hold her life in his hand—when all along, it had been the opposite.

He had been wrong about her in every possible way.

And anyway, she did not appear to have heard him.

"But you have a bigger problem," she was saying instead. "And I'm certain you won't think it inconsequential in the least."

She smiled, and he had an inkling that he was not going to like whatever she had to say at all.

Or, something in him whispered, in a voice he told himself he did not recognize as he had not heard it in so long, not unless it was a song, *you might well like it too much, Cyrus. And then what will become of you?*

But he could not entertain his mother now, not even in his own head.

He thought he might explode.

"Hope," he began. *"Omri—"*

But she would not be silenced.

Not even by that endearment that he had not said sardonically in quite some time.

"Congratulations, Cyrus," she said instead, with that steel beneath her soft tone that always told the truth about who she was. How had he let himself forget that, too? "I'm pregnant."

And that was when Cyrus understood that Hope had been the real storm all along, delivering him straight into his doom.

CHAPTER TEN

HOPE DIDN'T EXPECT Cyrus to throw her a baby shower. She wasn't *completely* delusional.

But she also hadn't expected that she would end the night in the dungeons.

Or that she would be the one to march down into the bowels of the fortress and lock herself in.

It had seemed liked a good idea at the time.

"You can come out of there any time you like," Cyrus growled from the other side of the bars. "This stunt of yours has gone far enough."

"When you say you're going to throw someone in your dungeons, I bet you mean it," she observed, then beamed a smile in Cyrus's direction. "So do I."

"You cannot throw yourself in a dungeon, Hope."

"I just did."

And there were other things she could have said to him then. Like the things she'd said a little too hotly upstairs, thinking she could poke at him the way she always did and he would explode the way *he* always did, and everything would end the way it normally did—

with him so deep inside her there would be no telling who was who.

But Cyrus had not imploded.

If anything he had looked as close to defeated as she'd ever seen him, and that had made her want to sob as nothing else could have. She'd felt her eyes well with tears, when she hadn't cried since her father died.

I would have locked myself away in the fortress dungeons if I had ever imagined these things could be possibilities, he had told her.

That was the first she'd heard of dungeons.

But she'd been focused on the rest of it. *Love isn't a disease, Cyrus. And I was the virgin when we met, yet even I knew that since we weren't particularly responsible about protection, a baby was always a possibility.*

That wasn't strictly true. She'd known, yes. But after a lifetime of not understanding why any woman would have sex with a man if she couldn't talk to him about protection, she'd found that she always had better things to talk to Cyrus about.

Somehow, the subject never came up.

I thought this was what you wanted, she'd said to him, all the while thinking that maybe it was what she'd wanted, actually. Way down deep where even she didn't know, maybe she'd longed for happy families all along.

And wasn't that a shock? When she'd long since thought herself far too worldly and sophisticated to believe in such fairy tales.

No, Cyrus had said in that gruff, low voice that hurt her to hear, his dark eyes so grim, so lost. *This was not at all what I wanted.*

Hope would have taken a moment to take stock of her new surroundings now, but it didn't require a moment. There was nothing here but bars on the door in front of her, a slightly raised hole in the floor she didn't care to consider too closely, and the cold stone floor.

This was well and truly an underground cell, as promised, with only the faintest sliver of a tiny window that she imagined might let in the sun in the morning.

If the sand didn't cover it first.

"At least the cell is dry," she said, cheerfully enough. Because she'd chosen this, after all. "It doesn't feel too warm or too cold, which is lovely. Honestly, Cyrus, if I hadn't spent the summer being fussed over in the harem, I might not have noted much of a change between my old flat in London and this. I'm happy to stay here for some time."

"Happy," he echoed. "And do you know, *omri*—? I believe you mean that."

Cyrus stared back at her as if he was looking for some kind of answer on her face. Hope kept her smile welded into place. Then he made a low sort of noise, wheeled around, and walked off down the hall. Back the way he'd come.

That was just as well, Hope told herself. Because she had been the one falling apart upstairs. She was the one who had come perilously close to an implosion.

Demanding the keys to his dungeons when he'd been implacable about leaving her here had felt like the only thing she could do.

Now, alone in her cell, Hope wondered for the first

time in her whole life if she was more like her mother than she'd ever believed possible.

Because if she wasn't mistaken, she'd just pitched what could only be called a scene. Though if ever there was a time to do it, she had to think being rejected by the man she loved after telling him she was pregnant with his child had to rank pretty high on the list.

She was sure that Mignon would approve.

Good job I'm not afraid of the dark, she told herself stoutly, now she was alone and there was only a bit of insipid light from out in the otherwise empty dungeon hall.

Then she took herself off to the furthest corner of the cell, which was to say, she took three steps, turned her back to the stone wall, and slid down onto the floor.

She listened to his footsteps disappear down that long stone walkway that she'd charged down as if she'd known where she was going. And when the last sounds of him faded and she heard that old iron door slam shut, Hope let herself breathe.

It had only been the other day when she'd realized that one of the reasons her time here had been so blissful was because there had been no monthly interruptions of that moody gargoyle that overcame her for a handful of days at a time.

And once she started thinking about that, she'd known.

She'd *known*, as if the knowing had always been there just beneath the surface, waiting for her to acknowledge it.

Hope had been lying in her alcove with one hand

pressed to the belly that still felt like hers when Yara, her favorite of all her attendants, had appeared in the archway, looked directly at the place where her hand rested, and lifted dark eyes filled with speculative wonder to meet Hope's own.

I d-don't know, Hope had stammered. *I only think maybe I might...*

The girl had whirled around and disappeared, but had come back swiftly. Hope had been standing by then, filled with a strange energy and a kind of indecision, too.

I don't want to tell him anything unless I know, she'd told the girl, maybe with too much of the things she felt in her voice, whatever those were. *I assume you must have your ways here. Ancient ways. Tea leaves, or some sort of magic drink, or...?*

The girl had held out a perfectly modern pregnancy test. *Or...* she'd agreed, with a smile.

They had known the truth within moments. It had been undeniable. Right there on the little stick.

You will tell our king tonight, the girl had said matter-of-factly, with more confident English than she'd exhibited all summer. Despite the lessons Hope had given all the women in the harem when they'd asked, then taught her a little of their language, too.

And perhaps there had been a different sort of knowledge in her gaze, too.

I will, Hope had agreed.

Though she was testing how that agreement tasted on her mouth. She didn't intend to share that with her attendant.

Our great lord will be the happiest of men, the girl had said, though she and Hope had continued to gaze at each other, engaged in a different sort of conversation altogether.

I'm sure he will be transported, Hope had replied.

And then had found herself wishing both that she'd taught the girl no English at all, or that she'd taught her a good deal more. Because she thought it would be better if she hadn't spoken up at all. Or, having done so, it would have felt much nicer if she could have gone down the list of pros and cons with the girl, as if she was any one of those old friends Hope had once had, long ago.

Instead, she'd ended up taking herself off to the dungeons.

She nodded off, there on the floor of the cell, which was significantly less comfortable than it looked. Which was saying something.

And then she woke up in a rush to a commotion out in the hall. She blinked in confusion at first, scrubbing her hands over her face and wondering if she would ever regain feeling in her bottom, then looked up. She expected to see Cyrus.

But instead, it was the women who attended her in the harem. And a selection of the guards. They all carried piles of things in their arms.

One of the older women barked at the guard outside the cell, the door was flung open, and in they streamed. Two of them came to Hope and clucked over her as if they'd found her in a garbage heap. The rest bustled this way and that until the cell better resembled the harem alcove room Hope had left up above. The cell was draped in luxury and not to be outdone, they had tucked Hope into the bed they'd made out of a pile of soft mattresses.

She almost sent them away, because she knew who must have ordered this.

But there was such a thing as cutting off her nose to spite her face.

"This is some kind of miracle," Hope breathed.

One of the older women said something in reply, and everyone—or rather, every woman—burst into laughter. Yara laughed too. But she sobered, patting Hope's hand. "She says that the curse of the King is that he must also be a man, and therefore given to foolishness like any other. So it is with our lord."

"Such a pity," Hope murmured, without as much guilt as she should have felt for not making sure they knew he hadn't put her here. "That even kings must be men in the end."

The women all laughed again. And only when they were all satisfied that their charge would sleep as comfortable a night as possible did they leave her to it.

And the next time Hope woke, the Lord and King of Aminabad was watching her from the other side of the bars.

Hope stretched as she sat up. "You're the one who encouraged me to believe in fairy tales, and look at what happened in the night! Don't you know? Anything is possible if you make a wish, Cyrus."

"It looks comfortable enough," Cyrus said quietly. "But there is a whole world out there, and I suspect you will grow tired of this cell soon enough."

And every time he came to visit her after that, the cell was even more pleasant. First there were thick rugs on the floor so her foot need not touch the cold stone. The women had erected something far more pleasant and civilized over that hole in the ground, then moved screens around it for privacy. On the walls, they hung priceless tapestries, and a series of tables to hold lanterns and the books they knew she liked to read.

One time he came she was eating a meal they'd brought her that was most decidedly not prison rations. Like gruel, she imagined, whatever *that* was.

She waved a roast chicken leg at him as she sat cross-legged on the comfortable floor that easily rivaled the luxurious space they'd used many times on the top of his tower. "Some people are queasy when they're pregnant," she told him, as if he'd asked. And it was easy to smile cheerfully when he looked so…glowering. "But not me. If anything, I'm that much more ravenous."

"Tell me how this happened," Cyrus said, his voice low and intense. Though she did not think he sounded *betrayed.* It seemed a crucial distinction.

"I think you know," she said. She patted her belly. "At least, I hope you know, with all your fancy education. Because I know, and I left school at sixteen."

"I don't mean the child."

And Hope studied his face, there on the other side of the bars that separated them. And she thought the bars made it all too clear what else separated them, that she had not paid enough attention to these last months.

"You don't want me to love you," she said softly.

"How could you?" he asked, sounding eminently

reasonable when the question was anything but. "We met when I kidnapped you."

"From a wedding I am just as happy to have missed. Let's not forget that part. Surely I should be the one who gets to decide if I feel traumatized by my own rescue."

But he only shook his head, looking at her as if despaired of her.

"This should not have happened," he said, in that same low voice that sounded like grief.

"You don't like that I'm in love with you," she said then, holding his gaze. "I understand that. But Cyrus. Have you asked yourself why?"

"This is the desert." He sounded almost astonished that she would question that. "It erodes everything it touches, especially love."

"Is that what you feel?" she asked him, too aware that the key to the cell was tucked under her pillow and she could go to him. Right now. She could let herself out and touch him, hold him, kiss that broken expression off his face. "Or what you were told?"

Cyrus did not reply. But he did not have to. She could see the truth all over his face, making that deep bronze face of his seem something like pale around the edges.

"Or is it worse than that?" she asked, almost too softly to hear. "Is that what he did to you here?"

"Enough," he muttered.

She didn't see him for two days after that. But that was good, in a way. It meant she had time to think.

Her life in the harem not only meant toiletries were provided—and usually applied by someone else—it meant that she was rarely on her own at all. Only when they left her to sleep for the night did she have a measure of solitude, though there was no door on her alcove. If she wasn't under her covers, there were always eyes on her.

The women and the guards were always, always watching, and even if she accepted that the watching was mostly benevolent—as her current situation suggested, since they'd outdone themselves making the cell into a luxurious retreat—it was still a lot for someone who'd spent most of her life feeling entirely alone.

Feeling it and usually actually experiencing it, too.

Now it all snuck up on her at once.

She'd found that she was pregnant, and instead of feeling terrified and overwhelmed, she'd been very much afraid that the overwhelming feeling that had raced around inside of her and threatened to swell up and burst free…was joy.

As foolish as that seemed, even then, when she hadn't known what Cyrus's reaction would be. Because she already knew she loved him. It had been a gradual dawning of awareness, and the way they made each other come apart only added it to it.

At first she'd thought she was simply addled by endorphins.

But she *liked* him. She liked how seriously he took his role here, so unlike so many of the men she'd met, who shrugged off responsibilities because theirs were inherited fortunes and needed no input from them. She liked how kind he was to his staff, always, no matter what they might have found him doing.

She liked the man his people thought he was, the man she learned about every day in the stories the women told her. About the time he had strode into an accident scene and took a child out of the line of danger. About how scared he had clearly been as a young boy, brought back here by his remote and rather terrifying-sounding father, but had shown such courage and bravery every day.

And if the women had sometimes heard the sound of muffled sobs at night, a lost boy missing his mother, they had never told the old King.

When the women had come to take her through her usual preparations for an evening with Cyrus that night, Hope had been happy to let them talk all around her, their voices rising and falling, as she considered the fact that she was carrying *life* inside her.

She had felt that only hours after taking that test, she was changed. Something in her had opened wide. No matter what happened, she knew what this felt like, now. She understood an entire new world of *possibilities.*

It had been easy to talk about things like this in an academic sense with men she was delighted she hadn't had to marry.

But now there was *a life* inside her, and Cyrus was the father. She had made love to him so many times that even thinking about him made her body warm. They had loved each other and the result was a life inside her, changing her even then. Changing her already.

She'd thought she'd understood a bit more about her own mother then, in a way she never had before. Not her fragility, her hummingbird flits and fancies, but those odd moments of power.

Like a mother tiger lives in her too, she'd thought that night. *Somewhere.*

Now, lying in her cell after having not seen Cyrus in two days, Hope found she understood Mignon even more.

Because her mother was not resilient. Not the way that Hope had been forced to become. Mignon's father had taken care of her. Then Hope's father had done the same and Mignon might have drowned her sorrows in too much wine and too many pills that were supposed to make her happy, or supposed to make her sleep, but in the end she had been loved.

She had been so loved. And she had been in love. Was it so terrible that she wanted to be loved again?

Hope had already been pretty certain that she was falling in love with Cyrus. How else could she explain how greedy she was for him? What else would make sense of the way she could not get enough, ever?

Knowing that she carried his child, and that she was fairly certain that he would not take kindly to that fact—but she was happy all the same—let her know there was no *falling* involved.

She had already fallen. And hard.

It was possible she had been half in love with him ever since he'd carted her out of that wedding chapel.

And the next time he turned up on the other side of her cell's bars, she regarded him solemnly.

From the freestanding copper bath where she had been soaking for some while, with bubbles in a foamy riot all around her and a bit of music playing in the background, too. For texture.

"How long do you plan to stay down here?" Cyrus asked.

More stiffly than the bars that stood between them.

"As long as it takes," she said. And when he only sighed, and did not ask to explain what she meant, she didn't know if she should be pleased. Or worried.

"I did not intend to get you pregnant, Hope," he told her, his voice still gruff—but laced through with that formality that never heralded anything she wanted to hear. She braced herself where she sat. "I understand I did not prevent it. I cannot account for my lapse. But you must see that this ruins everything."

She supposed he meant his plans. Her life in his palm and all the rest of it. The mighty desert and sand in all directions. The other women he told he would marry, though he had brought no others here.

Maybe all men were fools, as the old woman had said.

Or maybe it was that he thought love was a ruin all its own.

"That sounds like a you problem, Cyrus," she replied. She considered him and how he stood straighter at her tone. At, no doubt, the disrespect in her words—but she knew him. She knew he liked it when she talked like that. So maybe everything wasn't quite as ruined as he pretended. "And while we're talking about these things, I want my mother."

"Your mother?"

He sounded as if she'd requested a pit of poisonous snakes be thrown into her bathwater.

"My mother," she repeated, enunciating each syllable. "I'm pregnant. I'm going to become a mother myself and I'd like to take what solace I can in mine. And honestly? That you don't understand why that might be the case is everything that's wrong with you."

Something sparked in his dark gaze. "There is nothing wrong with me. As a matter of law. I am the Lord and—"

She waved a hand, dismissing him from behind iron bars in her cozy cell. "I'm a prisoner, Cyrus. You might not have put me in this cell, but you had every intention of jailing me in this fortress. Not only this summer, but for the next *year.* A prison is a prison no matter how big it is. All I did was make it obvious."

Then she tipped her head back, closed her eyes, and pretended to be asleep.

When she opened up her eyes again, he was gone.

Another few days passed. Hope assumed that he was off having a very kinglike temper tantrum somewhere else. Though usually when he took his trips, someone told her so. As if his staff was invested in her thinking well of him.

When what she'd thought was that their investment was what spoke highly of him.

Whatever he'd been off doing, he appeared in the dungeon on the fifth day, ordered the cell door flung open, and then bore her with great ceremony back up out of the dungeons and into the harem again.

"What's going on?" she asked him as the doors were

opened and Cyrus himself actually walked her into the harem courtyard.

He didn't answer. He merely extended out his arm toward the center of the of the pretty square. And took her some moments to stop blinking in all the bright and dazzling light that poured down from above. From the glare of the blue sky and the scent of all the flowers.

It took her a moment to accept that she had missed this place.

And another moment to make sense of the figure that stood there next to the fountain, not dressed like the other women at all.

Mignon. It was Mignon, who was already crying—leaving Hope to work very hard not to do the same.

They threw themselves into each other's arms, murmuring in a long stream about the time they'd spent apart, and so many apologies, and any other number of inanities that all meant the same thing.

I love you.

I missed you.

I love you.

Later that night when the guards came for her they found her sitting in the room in the harem that had been made up for Mignon. Hope rose from her chair, leaving her mother sleeping soundly. Still not quite believing that Cyrus had actually let her come here.

That he had gone and fetched her, according to her mother.

"It's amazing what good it does my soul to see her happy," she said when she'd been led up the stairs and out into a terraces of his bedchamber, with heat lamps blazing all around to keep the cold desert air at bay. "It's been a long while since I've seen her sleep without chemical help. And I owe that to you."

It felt strange to be with him again like this, but also familiar. Deliciously, marvelously familiar.

"I am sorry," Cyrus told her from where he stood near the rail, so stiffly she understood that he had not come to her on purpose. That he was even, perhaps, unsure of his welcome.

As if he was unused to the very words he used, come to that. If she thought back, had he actually said he was sorry the last time he had admitted he was wrong? All she remembered was losing herself in his arms.

She knew she should be mad about that. And yet she smiled at him, because she couldn't seem to help it. "You mean…because your pregnant wife felt she had no choice but to lock herself in your dungeon?"

"That," he said, inclining his head. His midnight eyes seemed to gleam in the dark. "Among a great many other things. Too many things to name, though I will if you wish it."

And once she would have laughed at that. She would have teased him into saying something or other that sounded like a list of wrongs, though it would never be finished. He would end up thrusting into her. She would end up forgetting.

They would do this again and again.

There was a part of her that was perfectly fine with that.

But things had shifted now. She was in love with him. She was going to be the mother of his child. And love Mignon though she might, she did not intend to end up like her mother. So destroyed by love that she'd been rendered weak because of it.

Hope was prepared to be many things, but she'd never been weak. She did not intend to start now.

There was the baby to think of.

"You have dungeons and palaces to match," she agreed, "though I've only heard tell of your palaces. I suspect you think that's the sort of thing you should apologize for, but it doesn't matter. If I were you, Cyrus, I would be far more worried about the little jail cell you keep right here."

His gaze was on her, as intently as ever, as she drew a little circle on her chest. Directly over her heart. "Because there's only one person who has that key, Cyrus. Only one."

He muttered something she didn't quite hear and then he closed the space between them, dragging her across the cushions and bearing her down into their soft embrace.

And there was some part of her that wanted to fight him. That wanted—

But even as she thought that, she also thought that she'd be punishing herself that way. He might deserve it, but Hope knew she certainly didn't.

And so she exulted in him instead.

In every stroke of his wicked tongue. In every glorious touch of his skin next to hers.

This had been the longest she'd gone without him since she'd met him and Hope felt as if she had a lifetime of pent-up hunger inside her.

They took each other in a blaze of passion, right there. They ate, not bothering to put clothing back on, and then he carried her to the bed, where they feasted on each other all over again. As if they were touching each other for the first time.

And that whole night, hour after hour, it was as if they bathed themselves in each other, in this passion that was only and ever theirs.

That was another thing Hope knew, without needing context or conversation. What they had between them mattered. It was special. If it was only sex, she would not be the only wife he kept in his harem.

If it was only sex, it wouldn't wreck them both like this.

It was near morning when she woke one more time to find his hands on her. Hope blinked as she looked around the bedchamber she knew as well as her own, now. And then to Cyrus, who had his hands on her belly.

Not attempting to stir her up into another display of that endless fire between them.

But for another, more intimate reason.

Because their baby curled up right there, inside of her. The baby they had made in love, though he might call it something else.

She knew better.

He glanced up, his midnight gaze finding hers and holding with such intensity that she caught her breath. Her stomach flipped over. Butterflies when they'd had each other already, too many times to count.

"I think this can work," he told her, his voice almost excruciatingly solemn. It made her ache. "You will have my child."

"I will," she agreed.

Because she might have locked herself in that cell, but he hadn't only sent furnishings and feasts. He had also sent in his doctors. She knew that everything was moving along as it should. As she was certain he did, too.

"You will have my sons, if the fates permit," Cyrus intoned, the way he did when what he was saying was *important.* In case she hadn't already been hanging on his every word. "I will make you my queen, Hope. There is no denying this passion between us and I have decided that I do not wish to deny it." He nodded then, though his gaze never shifted from hers. "I will allow it, Hope. And in so doing, it will perhaps become like any other duty."

And then he waited, as if he had offered her the world on a platter.

Or even a few sweet words.

"This is not the most romantic thing I've ever heard, Cyrus." Hope considered. "Then again, maybe it is. You haven't mentioned any dreary contracts yet. Or questionable activities. I'll give you points for that."

He frowned at her, then he withdrew his hand from her belly. He rolled up, moving so he could sit with his back to her and his legs over the side of the bed.

And that did not bode well.

Hope wanted to reach for him, but something about how straight he held his spine, then, made her think better of it. She crawled to the far edge of the bed, then stood. Then she went around to the foot of the bed to see if she could find her clothes.

And she had only just finished smoothing her silks back into place when he spoke again.

"All of these things are possible between us," he told her, his voice dark. Foreboding, she could not help but think. If not actively forbidding, too. He turned to look at her then, and there was something about those midnight eyes, so dark across the stirrings of the brand-new dawn outside the windows. It was suddenly difficult to breathe and it was nothing like butterflies at all. "But for this to work, Hope, you must never mention love again."

And Hope had really never felt more like her mother than she did at that moment.

Because everything in her wanted to say yes. *Needed* to say yes. She wanted to scream it out loud, because surely if he gave her all these things she wanted, himself most of all, love would come.

That was what she believed, in truth. That love made its own rules. That Cyrus did not need to believe in it. He did not need to feel it, though she didn't believe he didn't. That was the thing—love didn't require belief.

There was already a softening deep inside of her and a little voice—her mother's, she knew that, but then again, it was hers too—whispered, *Tell him whatever he needs to hear. Then love him enough for the both of you.*

And maybe she would have done exactly that, in a different life. If her father had lived long enough to tell her about the marriage he'd arranged for her and she had met Cyrus the way, perhaps, she'd been meant to all along. If all she'd known was that boundless love that had filled up and patched over every hole, and made certain each night that the day would come.

But she had lived through those other years, too. She had watched as her mother had tried her best to make men love her when they did not. She had watched her mother dash herself against those rocks again and again and again.

Still, everything inside her told her that this would be different. That *she* was different. That he was certainly like no other man she'd ever met, and surely all of that had to count for something.

She almost said yes.

God, how she wanted to say yes.

But instead she shook her head. "No."

His head tilted slightly to one side, as if he could not understand the syllable he had just heard. "What did you just say to me?"

"No, Cyrus."

Hope made herself breathe, then she made herself stand tall. She had been looking for a job her whole life, hadn't she? And now she had one. She would be a mother to this child inside her. She would be a daughter to the mother she had.

And she would be a queen to this man, but only if he was the King she needed.

Hope had taken on the wisdom of the desert in the course of her summer here, because the desert was everywhere. Its lessons were unavoidable.

And the real fairy tale, the one that mattered, was that a princess could become a queen with or without a man who was too foolish to know what was right in front of him. The desert was eternal. So too was love.

She wanted a man who could appreciate both.

"I have never been any man's whore," she told him, though the words hurt more than they should. "You know this. Why should I be yours?"

"Hope—" Cyrus began.

But she lifted a hand and silenced him, that easily. He did not need to tell her that she was the only one who would dare such a thing, because she knew it.

The same way she knew that this man, the King of the Aminabad Desert, was the love of her life.

Yet this was not a stunt. This was *life*. Her life, her child's life. And his life too, little though he might realize it.

"I won't," she told him, as regally as she could manage. "I would rather be back in the dungeon."

Then she made for the doors, throwing them open, and stalking through—paying no attention to the startled guards.

Hope did not go back to the harem. She walked herself straight back down to the cell she had left behind earlier, closed the door behind her with her own hands, and locked it tight.

Letting her silks fall where they liked.

Because she was perfectly prepared to stay where she was.

For as long as it took.

CHAPTER ELEVEN

CYRUS HAD TRIED REASON.

He had tried thundering his commands through the bars of the dungeon cell in the hope that might cow her.

He had tried rash promises. That he would take no other wives. That he would make a formal proclamation, not only declaring her Queen, but making it clear to the whole of the kingdom that this Lord of the desert would keep her even if she never gave him a son at all.

But for reasons that escaped him, she remained wholly unmoved by his every attempt.

Are you truly determined to give birth to our child in a jail cell? he had demanded at last.

All Hope had done in return was invite her mother into the cell with her, so that Cyrus had two pairs of reproachful golden eyes glaring back at him as if he had somehow disappointed them both.

When he should not have cared either way.

Her mother had dared to mutter something in French that she clearly thought he could not understand. He wished he had not.

Mother, that is not helpful, Hope had murmured

calmly. Also in French. Too calmly, to his mind. *I think you know perfectly well that he is in no way impotent, or we would not be in this position, would we?*

Cyrus had ground his teeth together, his jaw so tight that it hurt. He had clenched his fists, but he'd stayed on his side of the bars.

What I really think, Hope had said after a moment of studying him in a way he found disrespectful and outrageous in the extreme, *is that if you want something to happen with me and with our baby, you had better start with your own mother.*

He had refused, of course. What use had he for that accursed woman?

But whether he flatly refused or shouted his reasons why, his wife would not be moved.

So he stopped.

It took perhaps an hour before he found himself growling out orders to ready his plane and fly him north once again.

And that was how he found himself standing at the end of a winding, rainy lane, on a typically vile autumnal English afternoon.

Being England, it wasn't even a proper storm. It was just rain.

And it tore into him all the same.

He'd had his driver drop him a good mile or so down the drive, because he needed to clear his head. He needed to make sense of what was happening.

He needed to do this without all those *songs* in his head.

Because he, Cyrus Ashkan, Lord of the Aminabad

Desert, had returned to this benighted country to see the one woman he despised above all others because his wife—who he should also despise, but did not—had demanded it.

Even though he was still sorting through all those revelations he'd had about his father. Even though he was still reeling.

Hope had told him to come here and so he had, to this house where he had been held prisoner for so many years.

Although, a voice inside him whispered as he walked along the lane that became more familiar with each step, *how much of a prisoner were you really?*

Because he remembered his time here all too well, now he was here again. He had learned to say otherwise. And he had eventually said it so many times that he had come to believe it was true, in its way. That those dreams he sometimes had—of swimming in these ponds and rowing boats across the lake, running along the wooded paths and climbing the trees, as free as he liked—were just silly fantasies out of storybooks.

Instead of real memories of the way he had spent the bulk of his days here.

Not that any of that mattered now, he told himself grimly, and marched on.

The house sat on the little knoll it always had. But he was bigger now, and could only look at the small incline and remember how he thrown himself down it so he could roll and roll, laughing riotously because his mother had always joined him.

He had not thought of that in years.

He did not *want* to think of any of this, just as he had not *wanted* to face the terrible truths he'd finally understood about his father.

Because it was one thing to acknowledge that, secretly, he had always known that she was not quite the horror his father had claimed she was while he was still far away. It was one thing to accept all the ways his father had been cruel to her as well as to Cyrus himself.

He had found that contract, tucked away in the office here, like a final taunt.

While Hope conducted her dungeon sit-in, Cyrus had stood with his feet in the sand, allowing himself his own reckoning with a man who had been dead for years.

A man who had never deserved Cyrus's obedience, much less his respect and admiration. He'd won those one beating at a time.

He sighed as he walked, climbing up the old stone steps. He remembered that his mother might have worried about the state of her figure, as many women did and as she personally had to do for her job, but he had never seen her abuse herself as his father had claimed. Nor had he ever seen her use any substances harder than the same alcohol he knew his father had liked to drink, though his father liked to tell a different tale, making her out to be a monster.

Cyrus had never considered her a monster. Not while he'd lived here, and not after, when he visited her for the express purpose of breaking her heart.

It was that visit that sat heavily on him as he walked up to the great front door, feeling cold and damp and furious straight through.

But this time, not at his mother. He wanted to say that he was mad at a golden-eyed woman who was even now eating her way through his kitchens while reclining at her leisure in an overly luxurious dungeon but he knew better.

The person he was angry at, always and forever, was himself.

Cyrus took his time at the door before he reminded himself that he was a king, not a boy, and rang the bell.

He had loved ringing it as a child. And it was funny, the things a man could carry around inside himself without knowing. The exact sound of that bell. The way it echoed through the grand old house. The sound of footsteps in the hall and the way the great old door opened with a stout, deep sound.

He remembered all of that. It sounded inside him, like words to those melodies he'd tried so hard to make himself forget.

And then he found himself staring at the same butler who had been here when he was a child. The old man had to be halfway to the crypt, but he still managed to give the impression that he was looking down at Cyrus from a great height.

Even though he had shrunk to half his size.

"Master Justin," he said, which was not the impeccable courtesy Cyrus recalled. But then, why bother with the faultless address he surely knew when he could remind them both that he had known the boy Cyrus had once been. "I must tell you, sir, that no one in this house will take kindly to it if you are here to further abuse your mother's kindness."

"If you could take me to her, please," Cyrus replied. From between his teeth.

The old man glared at him for a moment so long that Cyrus wondered if he was going to have to take matters into his own hands—but then, at the last, turned on his heel with a hauteur that was meant to land like a slap, and did.

Cyrus found himself feeling more shame that he could remember ever experiencing before in all his days.

"You had better start with your own mother," Hope had said.

Had he known all this time that if he dared, this would be the reception he'd get? Or worse, that he would deserve it?

But he'd come all this way. And he was not a coward, despite all evidence to the contrary, so he continued.

He followed the old man deeper into the house and pretended he didn't recognize the place with every step he took. The rooms he had treated as his personal playground. The banister he had treated as his own, particular slide. The games of tag in and around precious artifacts, heedless of the fact that lords of the desert were not meant to enjoy themselves like grubby peasants, according to his father.

They were meant to conduct themselves with dignity in all things.

That desert he loved now, deeply and fully, had been a hard landing. He had been forced to change his own memories in his head to survive it, or he wouldn't have made it—not with his father so determined to claw out any hint of weakness in his only son.

It had been easier to pretend he'd hated it here. Safer, maybe.

In time he'd believed his own reframing.

Maybe that, too, had been survival.

But he cast the clamor of his memories aside as he was ushered, with freezing cold courtesy, into what he recognized as his mother's favorite drawing room.

He stepped inside, then stopped still.

Because she was there.

His mother stood at a window that looked out over the drive, and Cyrus realized she must have seen him coming.

She looked older too, even from behind. She was tall and willowy, still clearly *her* in every way that mattered, and he wanted to go to her more than he wanted to admit.

The last time he had hated that urge in him. He had wanted to claw it out with his own fingers. This time he did not quite dare approach her.

"Mother," he said, getting the words out even though he wasn't sure what there was to say. "I've come to you because—"

But the woman who had once graced every major magazine on the planet with her face, and who had briefly been one of the richest women in the world entirely because of her commanding presence, turned then and silenced him with a single glance.

From dark blue eyes far too much like his own.

Though hers were haunted.

And he knew without having to ask that any ghosts there were his fault.

"You have said quite enough over the years," she told him, in that quietly cultured voice he remembered so well. "I believe I'd like to take a turn."

"You don't understand," he started. "It isn't—"

"I love you, Justin," she said, stating it baldly. She did not drop her gaze, not even when she shook her head. "To me, you will always be the baby I carried in my body. The baby I made with your father, in love. The word he always hated most because he could not control it and so it made him feel weak."

When he had been eighteen she had tried to say something like this to him. She had called him by that name he had rejected for years then, too. Cyrus had refused to hear it.

He could almost see himself standing here in the corner of this very same room, shouting at her. *My father is the Lord of the Aminabad Desert,* he had thundered at her. *He has never known weakness, nor ever shall.*

But Cyrus wondered now if he had been that angry because she'd called him *Justin.* Because she'd made him remember and he'd been too concerned about chasing his father's approval back then.

About living up to all the harsh expectations his father had made sure he felt as if they were branded into his flesh. As if he could not be whole without them. As if they were as real as the bruises.

As if, he thought now, he'd had no choice but to hate his mother— for if he didn't, he would have to face what his father had done by stealing him away from her.

Cyrus was older now. His father had died a bitter man, with too many daughters for his liking and talk of a curse hanging over him. And he certainly would not have approved of this.

Of Cyrus coming back here of his own volition, a clear sign of weakness so great it might have killed his father if he had not already died.

But what Cyrus had learned from Hope was that he was not afraid of his weaknesses. On the contrary, he liked to indulge in them.

He understood more than he thought his father would like, if he were still here.

No man would react the way his father had unless, at heart, he was more afraid of what love could do to him than he was of what power would.

Because power was easy. It required nothing except greed, if you liked.

But love asked for everything.

Cyrus could not say he liked being asked. He had not reacted well.

Maybe he was more of a coward than he'd imagined.

And in the end, it came down to what he wanted more. The life his father had handed to him, wrapped up in a bow, but with entirely too many strings. Or the life that he saw in Hope's bright gaze.

A life where he was treated like magic and also a man. Where she saw who he was and all his many faults of arrogance and willful blindness, and forgave him anyway. Loved him anyway. Where there was always laughter and never that cringing, terrified awe that women had exhibited around his father. Where she not only made him smile, she made him imagine that he was not the creature of stone and silence he had long imagined he was. That he could make her laugh, too. These small, happy gifts lit up even an austere fortress in the desert. Even him.

And they made the harder parts of life seem brighter.

She did that. Hope did.

"Mother," he started again.

"I loved him," his mother told him in her same deliberate way, as if these were words she'd practiced in the hope of saying them someday. "And I know he told you a thousand stories of how that wasn't true, but I did. I would have loved him forever, but he wouldn't allow it."

Cyrus let out a breath, but he did not try to speak over her. He did not try to take control of this conversation. He let her speak.

And she straightened, there before him, as if she had been prepared to wilt instead.

He didn't like how that sat in him.

"And I might have accepted that, for your sake, but it became clear to me that he could not love anything," his mother told him. "He could not allow even the faintest hint of it into his dreadful little kingdom because I believed you deserved more than sand and stone. I wanted you to have a heart. I wanted you to love something, anything."

He wanted to tell her that he had, that he did, that he wasn't that furious youth who had come back here to denounce her. That he knew, now, that he had done that because it was the only kind of love his father recognized. That twisted inversion of it.

And because he had needed to believe what his father had told him, or he would have had to face what he'd lost.

God, what he'd lost.

And she moved closer, still holding his gaze intently. "And I don't care if you don't love me, Just—*Cyrus*. I don't care if you break my heart in a thousand pieces again and again. I'm your mother. I will love you enough for the both of us. I do."

As Hope would, Cyrus understood then in a rush and he hated it. For Hope. For his mother. For the creature he'd become that both of them thought it necessary.

When he was the one who had something to prove here, not them.

His mother stopped then, her eyes too bright, and seemed to recollect herself. Cyrus found his chest working overtime, as if he had done something more active than simply stand here, listening.

At last.

She inclined her head, looking almost perfectly composed. "I don't know what you have come to bludgeon me with today, my son. But you may go ahead. I only ask that you do so fully aware that I will love you all the same, whatever you say. Whatever your father told you, whatever you believe, I have always loved you. I will always love you. And nothing either he or you did or could do will ever change that."

And there were so many things that Cyrus could have said to that. So many ways he could have responded.

But instead he found himself moving toward her, like the boy he'd once been. And he could see how badly he'd hurt her when he saw the way she stiffened, as if bracing herself for attack.

That was the man he had let himself become. He could see that in her eyes, as she braced herself.

And he vowed that no matter what it took, he would not be that man again.

He would not be that man, that father, to his own child.

His own father was dead. And would stay buried.

When he reached his mother, he took her hands gently in his. He bent his head.

"Teach me how," he said.

And for the first time, he saw a crack in the armor she wore.

"Wh-what?" she stammered out.

"Teach me how you can love like that, Mother. Teach me how you do it."

He felt her tremble. He saw her eyes brighten more, though she did not allow a single tear to fall.

Cyrus wondered why it had never occurred to him that he might not have gotten all of his strength from his father's side after all.

Well. He knew why. But now he saw his mother plain, and he could not unsee it.

"My darling boy," his mother whispered, a joy too intense in her gaze, so sharp it was nearly grief. "I will teach you anything you wish."

And so she did.

He stayed with her that night and through the next day. They walked together on those lands he had told himself he'd forgotten. But he wanted to know her and the life she had crafted here in the wreckage his father—and he—had left behind.

And he could admit that the boy who had always loved her wanted to tell her what he had done and what he had learned, so she might know that what she'd given him might have been hidden—but it had never been truly lost.

Then, on the third day, he promised her that he would never stay away again, and took the lessons his mother had imparted to him home to his desert fortress.

And he ordered his men to bring his wife before him.

But not, this time, into his bedchamber. Not high on top of the tower, or hidden away in the baths.

Not even in the harem, which had been built for the King's eyes only.

This time, he gathered all his men and all the staff of the fortress, from the women in the harem who tutted at him to Mignon Cartwright herself, who studied him as if looking for a way that she, personally, might take him down. He believed that she might try.

And then, finally, when everyone was assembled, he allowed his men to bring Hope herself before him. In something slightly more modest than her silks, because while he was not his father, he was still a man. And he liked to keep what was his to himself.

Even out here with the sun beating down, making it impossible to hide.

"Oh, dear," said Hope as she walked into the center of the courtyard and stood there before him, looking undiminished and unafraid.

And more beautiful than any woman had the right to be.

She made him feel weak, but he understood that now. She made him feel mortal. As if he was nothing at all but a man.

And that, his mother had assured him, was the point.

Vulnerability is joy, if you let it hold you, she had said. *You'll see.*

And he had wanted that to be true, back in England in all of that damp and gray.

But here, in the unforgivingly clear glare of the desert sun, he knew it was. He felt it deep in his bones, that had not crumbled. He heard it like a song that he was no longer afraid to sing.

And more, he reveled in it, because of Hope.

He strode to meet her. And when she was within reach, he stopped. Turning slowly, there before his people, he stretched out his arms, inviting them all to look upon him.

"I stand before you, Lord and King," he said, and all of his people murmured the appropriate words in reply, bowing their heads. Hope stared back at him, her head unbowed. "But first, I am a man. A husband. And soon enough, I will be a father."

He turned fully, back to Hope.

And then, holding her gaze, he sank to his knees before her, smiling when he heard the mutters that ran through the crowd. "I kneel before you, the mother of my child. I kneel before you because I grant you that power over me that some call weakness, but that you and I know is far stronger than thrones or armies or ancient tales whispered down through the ages."

"Cyrus..." she whispered then, her golden gaze wide. "What are you doing?"

"This is the love of a king, *omri*," he said. And he used that word deliberately now, here in public where it could not be taken back. *Omri. My life.* So that all who heard it would know he meant it. So that she would. "I will always do my duty to my people, to my land. But my life, my heart, my soul—all of these are yours, Hope. There will always be a Lord of the Aminabad Desert, as long as there is sand to dance beneath the desert sun." All his people murmured their *hallelujahs* when he said this, as was tradition—but he kept going. "But as long as that lord is me, I will love you. As long as there is breath in my body and blood in my veins, I am yours."

He waited as she stood there, looking something like stricken as she gazed at him.

So Cyrus let his mouth curve, and did not quite incline his head. "If, that is, you will have me?"

And for a moment, he thought all was lost.

That he had taken this too far, with plots and harems and his regrettable reaction to the news he should have known was coming, that of course she would fall pregnant if he did not one thing to stop it—

I suspect you wanted not to think about it, his mother had said, too wisely. *So that you could force the issue. You are an Aminabad king, Cyrus.* And she had smiled. *You like a choice to feel like an inevitability. Preordained, if possible.*

But that didn't mean that Hope had reached the same conclusion. Or would.

She shook her head and stepped back, breaking his heart into pieces.

He thought of his own mother, who had loved long beyond any hope that it would be returned. Who had told him, in all seriousness, that even if he had never come back to her, she would have loved him forever. *Love is not about what does or doesn't happen,* she had said. *Love is about love, and I know you don't understand this, my darling boy, but it is its own reward.*

But here, in this moment, he understood.

Loving Hope had taught him what it was to be alive.

Not simply the brutal creature his father had insisted he become. He was a man grown, and he could make himself in his own image. There were already too many cracks in the stones his father had placed around his heart.

For one thing, Cyrus could not imagine caring at all if the child Hope carried was a daughter or a son, so long as it was healthy.

So long as he and this woman who had given him everything already could care for it together.

Cyrus knew he would still feel these things, because she had taught him how to feel in the first place, no matter what she said next.

He accepted this.

But that didn't mean he couldn't try to sway her.

"I love you," he told her, and he did not care if the whole of his kingdom heard him. "I love you like the sun loves the earth and I will continue to love you, even if you cast me aside. I loved you before I met you, building you up in my head. I loved you when I brought you here, when you defied me at every turn and confounded me because you would not cower and you would not become every wrong thing I imagined you to be. You would not bend, you did not break, and in so doing, you have taught me that there is no shame in either. You have taught me strength and you have taught me hope itself, like the beacon of it you have been and always will be. I was wrong about you in every possible way, and I am so glad you loved me anyway. And all of this will be true, *omri*, no matter what you say next."

And for a moment there was only the sun all around, the sky up above. The desert outside these walls where the sands were always shifting. Always waiting to take back what belonged to them. Filled with the ancient knowledge of the thousands of lives that had come and gone before his. And thousands more that would come after, then blow away again, sand into sand again.

All of those lives meaningless, he thought, without love.

As his father's had been.

Just as his had been without Hope.

"With, of course, some draconian custody arrangements, I assume," she said at last. "Should I decide that I prefer less sand, on balance, than you have shown me thus far."

But she said it all in that dry, amused tone that flooded him with relief.

And joy.

Cyrus let himself smile at her, heedlessly, and then

rose to his feet. "But of course," he said. "I am a man of great power and might, lest you are tempted to forget."

And what he wanted most was that smile of hers that took over her face now, and the way it made the bright desert day seem dim.

He wanted to talk to her forever. He wanted to fence words, and learn how to laugh as she did. He wanted to sink into each and every moment as she liked to do, so that all of it, all of life, was a sensual act.

But first, here and now, he needed more than that.

He moved forward and took her face between his hands.

"Hope," he managed to get out, to the only audience that mattered, "I love you. And I may not know how, but I can tell you this. There is nothing I cannot learn, and nothing I cannot do. My father made me a king. You made me husband. And I will make myself the man you deserve. I will make certain that I am worthy of the love you gave me so openly. When I could not even recognize it for the gift it was."

"And yet it is yours," she said simply. Truly. As openly as she ever had, because this was who she was. "It has always been yours."

"I will never deserve you," he whispered fiercely, bending his face to hers. "But I promise you this, *omri*, my beautiful life and my only Hope. I will never stop trying."

"I won't let you," she whispered back.

"Then it will be so, you and me," he told her, in the way he made all the proclamations in the land. "It will be love, as long as we live."

For he was a man of stone, fashioned by the desert sands and subject only to the whim of the winds that shaped them—and the woman who loved him and made him whole.

CHAPTER TWELVE

AND SO IT was that the mighty Lord of the Aminabad Desert became a great legend, hailed forever after as the King who changed everything.

For in this modern age, it was not war his people craved. Not the kind of wars he had been trained to fight by a man made of bitterness and bile.

What they wanted was joy, if they dared reach for it across the chasms of tradition and superstition.

Cyrus showed them how.

Hope gave him a daughter. Then a son a year later. Then one more of each.

"Not an army, I know," Hope liked to say. "Because we wanted a family."

And they raised them together, in ways men and women in Cyrus's country did not often do—especially when they were of royal blood. Cyrus sang them all the songs his mother hand sung to him when he was small. He played with them as his father never had with him.

He loved them, that was the thing, and they did everything together. The King and Queen did not like to be without each other, and so they traveled from region to region as a family. They spent a season in each, so that the whole of the country could know them.

And love them.

And learn from them that it was possible to live the way they did—in a marriage where love came first, vulnerability was championed, and brutality was never tolerated.

Not even when Cyrus turned over a stone and found such things in himself.

The children were raised by the whole of the land, so that there could never be any doubt that the great desert kingdom was ruled first by love, and only then by the power and might of its people, who knew exactly the character of those who would lead them.

Some even began to think that the eldest daughter might be their first ruling queen, in time.

Cyrus's mother came back to Aminabad, hesitant at first. But as she was not there to have her heart broken again and again, she found many things to admire about the kingdom. And, in time, to love.

She and Mignon struck up an unlikely friendship, and it was through her connections that Mignon met her second husband at last. A man who felt strongly that he had married above himself. A man who loved her, not as a trinket, but as a treasure, and cared for her all the rest of their days.

Cyrus's own mother had no wish to remarry. *I loved him,* she said simply, when Cyrus asked.

Instead, she became his children's favorite. She was often the person they loved more than their parents, who did insist on instilling in them rules and boundaries.

But as for Cyrus and his beautiful wife, his marvelous life in all ways, the balance always tilted toward joy.

Sometimes all there was of joy was her hand in his, holding on tight and refusing to let go.

That only made it more precious when it was easier, when both of them laughed themselves silly. When pride in their babies made them swell up as one. When the kingdom lurched its way along toward the kinds of change they'd thought they would only ever get to whisper about in the privacy of the quite modern homes they lived in, one in each region.

And whenever they could sneak away, they went back to that fortress in the desert.

Back to the harem, where the women would prepare her for his pleasure and they were free to feast on each other as they had at the beginning.

Recklessly. Carelessly.

And every year, more bright with love.

So that the legacy they left behind them, and in each and every one of their children, was that same bright joy they found in each other.

Love like the sun. Joy as eternal as the sands.

And knowing how to dance, however badly or without music, wherever the wind took them in between.

* * * * *

Caught up in the magic of
The Desert King's Kidnapped Virgin?

Then don't forget to look out for the next installment
in the Innocent Stolen Brides duet
The Spaniard's Last-Minute Wife
coming soon!

In the meantime, check out these other stories
by Caitlin Crews!

Willed to Wed Him
The Christmas He Claimed the Secretary
The Accidental Accardi Heir
A Secret Heir to Secure His Throne
What Her Sicilian Husband Desires

Available now!

COMING NEXT MONTH FROM

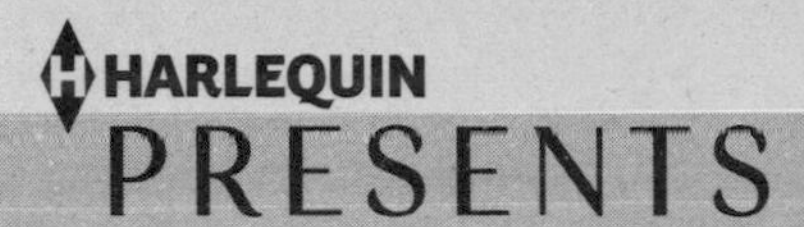

#4137 NINE MONTHS TO SAVE THEIR MARRIAGE

by Annie West

After his business-deal wife leaves, Jack is intent on getting their on-paper union back on track. He just never imagined their reunion would be *scorching*. Or that their red-hot Caribbean nights would leave Bess *pregnant*! Is this their chance to finally find happiness?

#4138 PREGNANT WITH HER ROYAL BOSS'S BABY

Three Ruthless Kings

by Jackie Ashenden

King Augustine may rule a kingdom, but loyal assistant Freddie runs his calendar. There's no task she can't handle. Except perhaps having to tell her boss she's going to need some time off...because in six months she'll be having *his* heir!

#4139 THE SPANIARD'S LAST-MINUTE WIFE

Innocent Stolen Brides

by Caitlin Crews

Sneaking into ruthless Spaniard Lionel's wedding ceremony, Geraldine arrives just in time to see him being jilted. But Lionel is still in need of a convenient wife...and innocent Geraldine suddenly finds *herself* being led to the altar!

#4140 A VIRGIN FOR THE DESERT KING

The Royal Desert Legacy

by Maisey Yates

After years spent as a political prisoner, Sheikh Riyaz has been released. Now it's Brianna's job to prepare him for his long-arranged royal wedding. But the forbidden attraction flaming between them tempts her to cast duty—and her *innocence*!—to the desert winds...

HPCNMRA0823

#4141 REDEEMED BY MY FORBIDDEN HOUSEKEEPER

by Heidi Rice

Recovering from a near-deadly accident, playboy Renzo retreated to his Côte d'Azur estate. Nothing breaks through his solitude. Until the arrival of his new yet strangely familiar housekeeper, Jessie, stirs dormant desires...

#4142 HIS JET-SET NIGHTS WITH THE INNOCENT

by Pippa Roscoe

When archaeologist Evelyn needs his help saving her professional reputation, Mateo reluctantly agrees. Only the billionaire hadn't bargained on a quest around the world... From Spain to Shanghai, each city holds a different adventure. Yet one thing is constant: their intoxicating attraction!

#4143 HOW THE ITALIAN CLAIMED HER

by Jennifer Hayward

To save his failing fashion house, CEO Cristiano needs the face of the brand, Jensen, to clean up her headline-hitting reputation. But while she's lying low at his Lake Como estate, he's caught between his company...and his desire for the scandalous supermodel!

#4144 AN HEIR FOR THE VENGEFUL BILLIONAIRE

by Rosie Maxwell

Memories of his passion-fueled night with Carrie consume tycoon Damon. Until he discovers the ugly past that connects them and pledges to erase every memory of her. Then she storms into his office...and announces she's carrying his child!